To the friends who have helped me through dark times.

Boy Seeking Band is published by Capstone Young Readers,
1710 Roe Crest Drive, North Mankato, Minnesota 56003
www.mycapstone.com

Cataloging-in-Publication Data is available on the Library of
Congress website.
ISBN 978-1-62370-853-5 (paper over board)
ISBN 978-1-62370-854-2 (eBook)

Cover illustration and design by Brann Garvey

Printed in China.
010348F17

BOY SEEKING BAND

BY STEVE BREZENOFF

Peachtree

Capstone Young Readers
a capstone imprint

PART
ONE

CHAPTER ONE

On the corner of Whatever Street and I Wish I Didn't Live Here Lane stands Terence Kato. He leans against a stop sign and watches as a school bus rolls by, brakes two blocks up, and lets on five kids the boy doesn't know. To be honest, Terence has no interest in ever knowing them.

By all rights, he ought to be on that bus, though. He should be seated next to some snot-covered, public-school kid who probably wouldn't know the circle of fifths if it rolled him over. But he's not.

Of course, it's also true that Terence's dad should be awake in time to drive his son to his first day at Franklin Middle School. But that's not happening either.

So instead, Terence pushes off the stop sign, hitches his bass guitar onto his shoulder, and heads around the back of his new house to fetch his bike.

"Later, Dad," Terence says to the drab, little rent-a-home as he rolls away. With every bump, stop, and practically every pedal, the bass guitar bounces hard against his back like some sort of punishment. But he has to bring it. First of all, he preregistered for the after-school band program and couldn't show up to the first day without an instrument. Second, wearing a gig bag attracts attention — the kind of attention he'll need if he has any hope of starting a band at Franklin, like the band he had back at Hart Arts, and entering the battle of the youth bands in the spring.

As Terence pulls up to the bike rack, which is full, he hears a school bell ring. He quickly chains his bike to a No Parking sign and runs inside.

The halls are quiet. Empty. He's late.

Inside the school's front office, a man behind the counter stares at a computer screen and speaks quietly into a headset. "Excuse me?" Terence says. The man doesn't look up.

Terence adjusts the strap on his gig bag and notices a surly-looking girl slouching in the metal chair behind him. She has dark skin, short hair, and a suspicious golden piercing in her nose. He's pretty sure she's staring at him, probably plotting when to knock him over the head and take his phone and wallet.

That's what they do in public schools: they beat you up and steal your stuff.

"Um, excuse me?" Terence repeats, trying to get the man's attention by waving his schedule around noisily. "It's my first day, and I'm late. I don't know where I'm supposed to be."

"He won't help you," says a voice behind him. Terence doesn't turn around, but he knows it's the scowling girl. "All day, every day, he's on that phone, doing who knows what, ignoring every student that walks in here."

Terence still doesn't turn around. "Did I ask you?" he mutters under his breath.

"No," the girl says. "But I'm a very generous person, so I'm helping you anyway."

"How are you helping me right now?" Terence asks, and he finally turns around to find the girl standing right behind him.

She's taller than him, which is nothing new. The Katos are a short family, but Terence's dad assures him that he'll have a growth spurt any day now and catch up — at least to the girls. Although Terence doubts he'll ever catch up to this particular girl.

"Let me see that," she says, snatching his schedule.

"Hey!" Terence says, but the girl turns around and blocks him from getting the paper back while she reads it.

"Terence Kato," she reads aloud, and then says over her shoulder, "Aren't you a little short to be an eighth grader?"

"Give it back."

"OK, OK," the girl says, finally handing him the paper. "Anyway, you missed advisory, but your first hour is in the same room. I can show you — if you want help."

Terence glares at her a moment and then glances at the man behind the desk, who still hasn't looked up.

"Fine," Terence mutters, and then even more quietly, "Thanks."

"No problem, Terry," she says. "I'm Meredith Carson, by the way. But you can call me—"

"Merry?" Terence interrupts as he follows her out of the office.

"Eddie, actually," she says. "Anyone calls me Merry, I knife 'em."

Terence flinches. Eddie laughs.

"I'm kidding, newbie," she says and then adds, "Or am I?

Terence isn't sure, really.

Eddie laughs again. "I take it from that Cadillac

strapped to your back you'll be joining our esteemed band?"

"It's my bass guitar!" Terence explains, his voice going higher and louder with excitement. "Are you in the band? What do you play?"

"Easy, eager beaver," Eddie says. "You know band class isn't until *after* school, right? It's extracurricular."

"I know," Terence says. "But my bass didn't fit in my locker, and I didn't know where else to put it."

She sizes him up. "Bet you would, though," she says. "Fit in your locker, I mean."

Terence feels his face go hot as she leads him around a corner. They head up to the school's second floor, and she stops in front of the first door: 212.

"This is your room, band boy," she says. "Have fun." With that, she leaves him standing in front of the closed door to his first public-school class since fifth grade.

He sneaks a look in the window. The tables are set up in clusters of four. Walking among the tables with her hands behind her back is —

Terence takes a quick look at his schedule: Ms. Hardison, his new math teacher.

"OK, you can do this," he whispers to himself as he leans on the wall next to the door. "Of course, if everyone in there is as nice and 'helpful' as *Meredith* was, this might be the worst hour of my life."

Suddenly, the door flies open and Ms. Hardison pokes out her head. "Will you be joining us this morning, Mr. Kato," she says, "or do you have a soliloquy to rehearse out here?"

"Oh, um . . . ," Terence mumbles, not because he doesn't know what a soliloquy is; Hart Arts had a renowned drama department. In fact, Polly Winger, the singer from his band at Hart, had been one of the department's top stars, even though she was only in eighth grade.

Terence missed his old school and his old life. But most of all, he missed the Kato Quintet. They were his best friends and the best band at Hart Arts. Sure, they were only miles away, but they might as well have been on another planet.

"Sorry," Terence finally says. "I had trouble finding the room."

Ms. Hardison steps to one side and holds the door open for him, smirking. "Welcome to Franklin Middle," she says as he passes, dodging the top of his gig bag. "What *is* that?"

The class laughs as Terence finds an empty desk in one of the clusters. "It's my bass guitar," he says. "It didn't fit in my locker."

"Just lean it in the corner," Ms. Hardison says, not bothering to hide her contempt for Terence's extra baggage.

Terence obeys and then slumps into his seat. His cluster-mates don't even look at him.

CHAPTER TWO

Terence's first day at Franklin Middle is as long and arduous as the first five minutes. Without Eddie as a tour guide, he's late to every class — even lunch. The one brief moment of pleasantness during his day is Music.

The teacher, Mr. Bonn, plays piano for forty-five minutes straight, practically, and the students sing with varying degrees of enthusiasm. To be honest, Terence is probably somewhere in the middle, and even the most enthusiastic singers in the room aren't nearly as good as Polly.

Almost no one is, Terence thinks as Mr. Bonn takes a brief pause between the end of the Beatles' "Here

Comes the Sun" and the start of A Great Big World's "Hold Each Other."

Terence and Polly did "Hold Each Other" in rehearsals once, long ago — six weeks ago, in fact. Terence did the rap. It was hilarious.

But Music class is less than an hour of Terence's first six-and-a-half-hour day, and Music alone cannot save it.

At 3:45, Terence hurries along Franklin Middle's back hallway. It slopes downward into the cooler underbelly: the basement, home to the school's utility room, storage, and "important" departments like Fine Arts and Music. He can hear a handful of other players warming up, and though they don't sound like half the talent he knew back at Hart Arts, it's still music to his ears.

Terence's heart races as he picks up his pace. He's almost jogging by the time he finds the orchestra room and hurries through the double doors.

Everyone stops and looks up at him: the stranger with the gig bag on his back.

"Um, hi," Terence says, carefully pulling the bass from his shoulder and holding it in front of him like a shield. "This is band, right?"

The dozen or so students gape at him, their saxophones, trumpets, and drumsticks stuck in limbo between being played and being set down.

"I'm —" he starts to add.

15

"Terence Kato!" says a booming voice.

"Yes?" Terence says, and then spots a giant man striding toward him from the back of the room. The man is easily six and a half feet tall and nearly as wide. He wears a walrus-like mustache, a brown corduroy suit that he's managed to sweat through, and a pair of thick, oversized eyeglasses.

The man wipes his hands on a cream-colored chamois as he thunders across the room like a walking tree. "We've been expecting you."

Terence glances again at the agape band members. "You have?"

"I'm Kenny Bonk," the giant man booms, "and of course!" He drops the chamois and walks back to the black metal music stand that serves as his conductor's podium. "Join the group. I see you brought your bass."

Terence nods.

"Didn't fit in your locker, did it?" calls a boy from the risers.

Terence looks up and spots him, a big baritone sax leaning on his hip.

"Mine either," the boy says, patting the sax's curved, shining top.

"That's Jordan," Mr. Bonk says. "You'll meet all the players, but for now we can get started. You're running a little late?"

"A little," Terence admits. He spots a bass amp beside the risers and makes a beeline for the chair closest to it, unzipping his gig bag as he goes.

"You can store your instrument here," Mr. Bonk says, "if you don't want to carry it back and forth each night. But you strike me as the kind of player who likes to practice every night. Am I right?"

"Um, yeah, I guess," Terence admits, but his face goes hot as he goes on, "But I have another bass at home I'll use to practice."

"Ah!" Mr. Bonk loosens his knit tie. "Life in private school, eh?"

Terence feels the eyes of his bandmates on him as he plugs in and fiddles with the amp's knobs.

Mr. Bonk pulls off his sweat-drenched jacket and tosses it aside. His undershirt is soaked through as well. "Let's start with 'Don't Mean a Thing,'" he prompts the class.

Terence actually smiles as he checks his tuning. The song is a Duke Ellington classic, perhaps the standardest standard of all jazz standards. Terence could play the bass part in his sleep. He probably has.

The rest of the band members, though, shuffle through sheet music, fuss with their stands, and look up at Mr. Bonk. The song often starts with just a piano intro, but this jazz band has no piano, and the sheet music probably comes from an arranger who specializes in school-band music, which means keeping things simple and plain.

"And a one, and a two," Mr. Bonk announces, raising his baton. When he enthusiastically lowers it with a strong jerk of his head, the band leaps into the song with all the swing and vivacity of a bowl of cold spaghetti without sauce. Even without melted butter.

Terence keeps his head down and runs through the bass line, but it's difficult playing a version of "It Don't Mean a Thing" with surprisingly little swing.

When the song is over, Mr. Bonk pauses for a moment, then looks at Terence and smiles politely.

Here it comes, Terence thinks. *He'll tell me how great I am, and how lucky I was to go to Hart for a few years, and I'll be all embarrassed. Just try to smile.*

"Mr. Kato," Mr. Bonk booms. "The others and I have been practicing 'Don't Mean a Thing' for a few weeks now from the sheet music provided. It would really help us if you could stick to the bass line as written."

"Thanks, I —" Terence starts, but then catches himself. "Wait — what?"

"There's a copy under your chair," Mr. Bonk points out, "along with the rest of our repertoire."

Terence reaches down and finds a short stack of

sheet music. "It Don't Mean a Thing" is right on top. Under that, "A Night in Tunisia," "Here's that Rainy Day," and "Manteca."

They're all classics. Terence would in fact love to be in a jazz band that played those numbers. Unfortunately, it happens to be *this* jazz band.

For the next forty-five minutes, the Franklin Middle School jazz band plods through their set list, a couple of times each song, and Terence nobly plucks along with them on his song-sheet-appointed bass line.

The exercise is utterly exhausting, and when it's over, Terence unplugs and packs, leaving his bagged bass in the back room per Mr. Bonk's instructions. Then he hurries from the music room amid stares from the rest of the band.

The basement halls are empty, and the school seems darker now. His footsteps echo as he struggles to recall the way back up to the main floor and the school's front doors.

"I think it's this way," Terence mutters, jiggling his keys, anxious to get back to his bike, unlock it, and ride home.

No, not home. *Just* house, Terence thinks. *That place will never be my real home.*

Terence turns right. *It must be this way.* Then he turns left and finds a stairwell, but the double doors are locked. He goes straight, then turns left, and then left again — another dead end at a locked, black, unmarked door.

"Great," he says, thumping the locked door with his fist. Then he adds, "Thanks a lot, Mom," though he knows none of this is her fault.

Terence slides down the wall and lets his book bag fall to the floor beside him. "Sorry," he whispers, an apology to his mom. He misses her still; he will forever, he sees now. Right after she died, Terence imagined that the missing — the pain he felt immediately after her death — would eventually stop, like getting over a very bad cold or something.

Turns out, mourning doesn't work that way. After six months, the pain is still like a tickle in his throat, ready to become a full-on flu at any moment.

Terence sniffs back tears and readies himself to find a way out of this middle school maze. But as he does, a faraway voice rises in the silence of the basement.

A girl's voice — singing.

For a moment, Terence sits frozen, too stunned to move. A single tear stalls in the corner of his right eye as if it too is caught up in the reverberating voice: *"Maybe . . . I should have saved those leftover dreams."*

A split second later, Terence leaps to his feet, wipes the swollen tear from his eye, and grabs his bag. It knocks against his leg as he runs up the hall, desperately seeking the singer. Instead, Terence finds abandoned hallways, echoing with vibrato and spinning him in maddening circles.

Before long, he's back at the orchestra room, but now the double doors are locked, the lights are off, and no one's around. Terence pauses a moment, his back against the locked doors, and tries to get a fix on the voice, but it quickly fades, and before long he can't tell if he hears it all, or if it's just an echo in his mind: *"Funny, that rainy day is here."*

And a moment later, silence.

This time, when Terence steps away from the orchestra room, he winds through the basement hallways and finds the ramp right away. In moments, he's on the first floor and at the front door, amid the cacophony of extracurricular students, basketball players and cross-country runners, after-school advisors, and office-hour department heads.

Terence pushes past all of them and through the front doors into a cloudburst, and though in moments he's drenched, he doesn't care. His bass is safely inside, after all. Besides, at the moment, he's more concerned that the No Parking sign, twenty paces down the sidewalk from Franklin Middle School, no longer has a bike chained to it.

Still, he drudges through the rain and grabs hold of the signpost, as if testing its very existence.

"Hey, Terry!" comes a girl's voice from behind him, one not nearly as spellbinding as the vocalist in the basement.

Terence turns around, knowing full well who he'll find standing just inside the open door. "Merry Eddie," he grumbles.

"You miss the late bus, new kid?" she calls through the rain at him as he plods through puddles back to the door.

"My bike was stolen," he says, though that has nothing to do with the late bus, which he didn't know anything about until this moment. Besides, he's not about to admit he got lost in the basement. He drops his bag as he steps through the door she holds open for him.

"Nah, not stolen," she says. "Impounded. You're not allowed to chain up to signs."

Terence slides down the locker closest to the door and pulls out his phone. "Now you tell me," he says as he selects Dad from his contacts.

"Aw," Eddie says, sliding down next to him. "You'll get it back. Don't worry. They'll make you fill out a form in the morning."

"Who?" Terence says.

Eddie nods toward the main office. "Them."

"Great," Terence says, recalling his experience in the office that morning.

After the fifth ring, Dad picks up. "Hello?" he says in a familiar, groggy voice.

"Dad?" Terence says. "Were you sleeping?"

At the same moment, a tall boy Terence recognizes from jazz band steps up to him and Eddie and says, "All right, I'm ready. Let's go."

"No," Dad says, forcing cheery wakefulness into his voice. "No, of course not. Where are you?" And a moment later, "Did I miss pickup? I'm sorry —"

"No, Dad," Terence says. "I'll explain later, but can you pick me up?"

"See ya, Terry," Eddie says, getting to her feet.

"Wait a second," Terence starts.

But Dad interrupts him, and Eddie and the boy disappear through the front doors. "I'll be there right away. I just have to —"

"Get up and get dressed?" Terence finishes.

Dad sighs. "Gimme a break, kid," he says. "I'm doing my best."

Terence takes a deep breath and stands up. "I know," he says, looking through the glass doors. For a moment, the rain has stopped.

CHAPTER THREE

Dinner that night is what Dad calls FFY: "Fend For Yourself." It used to be something special, back when Dad *and* Mom called it that. Basically, Terence could make anything he wanted — mini pizzas, mac and cheese out of the box, or PB&Js — and Dad would get the night off from cooking.

But Dad has had the night off from making supper for months now, and FFY isn't cute anymore. Terence takes his mini pizzas — English muffins topped with American cheese and ketchup — to his tiny bedroom and dumps his homework onto the bed.

None of it is music homework, but Terence pulls his bass out from under the bed, and plugs in anyway.

He turns the volume down, fiddles with the EQ, and runs through every scale he can think of until he nearly falls asleep.

The next morning, Terence shovels down his bowl of cereal, doesn't bother to wake Dad, and takes his chances on the bus. His stop is one of the first, so he manages to snag a seat to himself in the middle: the invisible section of the bus.

In the middle, you're not some butt-kissing weirdo who wants to sit right up close and personal with the bus driver, but you're also not interested in the hijinks, spitballs, and phone videos being shared in the back.

Two stops later, though, to Terence's surprise, someone shoves in his book bag and sits down next to him. Terence doesn't look up. He just pushes against the window, stares outside, turns up Joni Mitchell's *Hejira* on his noise-canceling headphones, and hopes it's clear that he's not interested in making friends.

For a minute, his plan works. After all, most people climbing onto this Franklin Middle bus aren't out to develop new relationships first thing in the morning. But soon his new seat neighbor grabs his arm and gives him a shake.

Terence looks down to find long fingers wrapped around his forearm, adorned with cheap, quarter-machine rings. The nails are painted every color of the rainbow and chipped. He's not surprised when he lifts his eyes and find's Eddie's expectant face, her lips moving in mock frustration desperately saying *something* over and over.

Terence rolls his eyes and pulls off his headphones in the middle of the title track — his favorite. Eddie's mouth keeps moving, silently, and slowly bends into a smile.

"You're hilarious."

"Sorry," Eddie says. "Couldn't resist." She nods toward the headphones. "Can I listen?"

Terence shrugs and hands over the headphones. Eddie puts them on, listens for a moment, and then says in a way-too-loud, headphone-wearing voice, "What the heck is this?"

Half the bus turns around to look at them. Terence grabs back his headphones. "It's Joni Mitchell," he says, shrinking lower in the seat. "Keep your voice down."

"Sorry, sorry," she says. "It's weird. Are you weird?"

"Sure," he says, hanging the headphones around his neck as he switches off the music. "I'm super weird. You should probably sit somewhere else."

Eddie laughs, and the bus jerks and screeches to a stop at the curb in front of the school. "See you, weird Terry," Eddie says as she practically leaps out of the seat.

Terence watches as she catches up with a boy — the same boy she left school with yesterday. The boy glares at Terence and, Terence swears, growls.

Terence thinks about ditching jazz band that afternoon. He wonders whether remaining a member of such an unfocused, untalented group would be detrimental to his playing in the long run. Two thoughts stop him from skipping: One, what if he never gets a band together? He'd have no one to play with except himself. And two, if he goes to band practice there's a chance that he'll find the girl with the echoing voice, the voice he needs for his band.

Terence arrives on time this afternoon, and while he unpacks his bass, he glances up at the sax player — it's the kid who picked up Eddie yesterday and escorted her off the bus this morning. He doesn't know this guy, but it's a safe guess that he's Eddie's brother. If Terence knows just one other student at this school — and he does know *exactly* one other student — it's Eddie.

Surely her brother will be willing to talk to him?

"Hey," Terence says as the bigger boy slips on his saxophone's mouthpiece and tests the reed quietly.

The boy looks up, his eyebrows furrowed and his lips tight around the reed of his sax.

"Hey," Terence tries again. "You know any singers?"

The boy pulls the mouthpiece out a fraction of inch, opens his mouth as if he might speak, but then instead draws in a huge breath and starts playing the opening bass line of Pink Floyd's "Money."

Terence stands there a minute, anticipating a genuine response, but when the boy closes his eyes — like he's really feeling the music — Terence gives up and goes back to his bass.

The jazz bands runs through their repertoire again, each number twice, until it's 4:30 and the late buses are due to leave. Terence is the quickest to pack up.

He sprints from the room into the cavernous basement hallways — and smack into Eddie. He knocks a cup of coffee from her hand, sending the chocolaty-brown liquid splashing to the ground.

"Whoa, Weird Terry!" she snaps. "Watch it."

"Sorry!" Terence says. "I was hurrying and —"

Eddie crouches and drops a handful of paper napkins on the spill. "It's fine," she says, though from the tone of her voice, he can tell it's anything but.

"Did I get your boots?" he asks. It's hard to tell because they're a little worn — in a cool way, of course. "Your pants?"

"It's fine," she repeats. "You can owe me for the coffee. And go get some paper towels."

Terence scans the hallway and spots the nearest boys' room. "On it," he says, dropping his book bag against the wall and taking off down the hall.

The restroom is a mess. The paper towel dispenser is not only empty but knocked clear off the wall. Thinking quickly, Terence bangs open the stall, pulls loose a big handful of toilet paper, and hurries back to the scene of the collision.

Eddie is gone.

Terence's bag leans against the wall a few feet from a pile of mocha-soaked napkins. He drops to his knees beside the remaining mess and wipes at it with the toilet paper, which quickly disintegrates in his hands. Terence sighs, gathers the mushy mess, and tosses the whole wad away in the boys' room trash can.

When he gets back to his bag and throws it onto his shoulder, the echoey voice from the day before suddenly returns: it's clearer today, closer — even nearby. This time the song is "It Don't Mean a Thing (If It Ain't Got That Swing)."

Terence brightens at once. He sprints up the nearby ramp and rounds the corner. The voice is so close.

At the top of the ramp, two backlit figures walk away from him toward the sunlight of the main floor: he is tall and lurching, like a half-ape; she is not quite as tall, and lean-looking and strong. And she's singing.

"Wait!" Terence calls up the ramp as he runs. "Wait up, you two!"

They stop and turn, and Terence still can't see their faces because the setting sun is like an orange and pink spotlight behind them, shining right into his eyes.

"Was that you?" he says, squinting and shielding his eyes, as he looks at the girl. "Were you just singing?" He looks over his shoulder into the basement. "Back there?"

The girl seems to glance at the boy beside her as Terence moves up the ramp toward them. Something clicks then, only an instant, before the angle of the sun changes so he can clearly see who's standing at the top of the ramp.

"Eddie?" Terence says, and beside her, the growling saxophone player from jazz band.

"You following me, Weird Terry?" Eddie asks. She doesn't look amused — or flattered.

"Who is this guy?" asks the big guy. Terence decides it must be her brother.

"Oh, some new kid," Eddie says, glaring at Terence. "He's harmless."

Terence swallows his pride and asks again: "Was that you singing in the basement a minute ago? 'Don't Mean a Thing'?"

She shrugs one shoulder. "Yeah, so?"

"Can I talk to you a second?" Terence asks, and off her brother's ice-cold stare adds, "In private?"

Eddie sighs, and then says to her brother, "Don't let the bus leave without me."

He growls but turns and walks toward the front doors, where the late bus is probably already idling. The bus is Terence's ride home too, since his bike is still in the hands of Franklin Middle School's powers-that-be.

"So what's up?" Eddie says, striding down the ramp to meet him. "And make it quick."

She stares at him with the patience of a hungry lioness being kept from her meal — and Terence feels like that meal.

Terence takes a deep breath. "Look," he finally says, closing his eyes and clenching his teeth, "I'm new here. You don't like me. I get it. I'm not out to make friends."

"Wow," Eddie says, and Terence goes on.

"I'm hopefully only here a few months, after all. But there is one thing I need to survive even that long, and that's a band."

"A band?"

Terence nods. "I play bass," he says, "and a few other things. I'm open as far as genre and lineup, but there's one thing I'll need, and that's a great singer. You're a great singer."

"I know," Eddie says, still unsmiling.

"Um," Terence says, because he kind of thought that would fluster her at least a *little* bit. "So what I'm asking is . . ."

"I know what you're asking," Eddie says as she backs away, up the ramp. Her brother has appeared at the top again to glower at them. "You want me to join your band, which doesn't exist yet."

"Yeah," Terence says, though she's managed to make it sound silly.

Eddie reaches the top of the ramp and turns her back on him. "I'll think about it," she says.

"I need you!" Terence calls after her as she and her brother walk off. "Um, that didn't come out right."

Her brother snarls over his shoulder at Terence. Eddie calls down the ramp, "You better get on the bus. It won't wait." With that, she and her brother vanish down the hallway.

"No, thanks!" Terence calls after them, though he's sure they can't hear him. "I'll get a ride . . . somehow." The thought of getting onto the bus with her after that awkwardness makes his stomach turn, so he pulls out his phone and calls Dad to wake him.

He picks up after the fifth ring. "Terence?" he mumbles, the sleep still in his voice.

"Dad," Terence says as he climbs the ramp toward the front door. He watches the bus pull away. "Remind me again why Mom didn't have life insurance."

Dad sighs. "You need a ride?"

"Yeah."

"Ten minutes," Dad says, and the phone clicks off in Terence's hand.

CHAPTER FOUR

First thing the next morning, Terence heads to the main office to try to get his bike back. Eddie's not there, and Terence idly wonders why she was there on his first day. Did she get in trouble a lot?

The man who ignored Terence the other morning is back at his desk — or maybe he never left his desk — talking quietly into his headset.

"Excuse me," Terence says, leaning a little on the counter. "My bike was confiscated a couple of days ago."

The man glances oh-so-briefly at Terence, but he doesn't say anything to him. He doesn't even pull off his headset as if he plans to listen to anything the boy says.

"I didn't know you're not allowed to chain up bikes there," Terence goes on.

The man ignores him.

"Is there a form I need to fill out, or . . . ," Terence says, but the question is drowned out by the sound of the bell to start advisory period.

The man looks up at Terence, points at the bell on the wall, and goes back to his call.

"Thanks," Terence says. "Thanks a lot."

The morning goes well enough, certainly better than his first morning. Terence is beginning to get a feel for the rhythm of this school — so different from Hart Arts.

At Hart, the core classes — like math, language arts, and science — were reserved for rotating classes after lunch.

Terence spent all morning before lunch in one classroom, with music instructors and other students majoring in music performance and theory. The room contained a pair of pianos, a range of percussion instruments, brass, woodwind, strings, and any other instrument you can imagine — there and for the playing.

Many mornings, Dr. Orderall declared an hour as free-play, and it wasn't the free-play he had in kindergarten. It was spontaneous rock trios blasting through hard-rock covers, wild jazz quintets riffing on a Gershwin melody, or even a string quartet swaying to Bach.

At Franklin Middle School, Terence is pretty sure a morning like that might be so off-the-wall that even the man in the office would hang up his phone and come out from behind the desk just to see what the heck is going on.

Still, by lunch on his third day at Franklin, Terence understands how the school works. The classes are, for the most part, entirely boring, but they keep the classes short so students can tolerate the boredom. That makes sense.

Earlier this morning, Terence didn't feel like making lunch for himself — and Dad was still asleep on the couch — so he's stuck with the hot lunch. He lines up.

"So, I've been thinking about it," says a familiar voice behind him.

Terence turns and finds Eddie leaning against the wall. "About what?" Terence says, though he knows she means his band that doesn't exist yet.

"You know you don't have to get the hot lunch," she says, rolling along the wall on one shoulder as the line shimmies up.

"OK," Terence says. "That's not what I thought you'd been thinking about."

"It's not," Eddie says. "But, I mean — least I can do. You should skip this — what is it today? Pot roast? — and hit the snack bar instead."

"What's the snack bar?" Terence asks.

Eddie rolls her eyes. She has very big eyes. "Come on," she says, taking his hand and pulling him out of the line.

She leads him in between tables and around the corner.

"I . . . ," Terence begins, gaping at the crowded corner of hidden tables, "had no idea this was here."

"That's my fault, actually," Eddie says. She takes him past the tables to a doorway on the far side. A sign hanging above it reads "Snack Bar."

"Whoa," Terence says, because there's a bagel line, a pizza line, a fryer line, and racks of chips, fresh fruit, and premade sandwiches and salads.

"Right?" Eddie says. "No reason to eat the slop from the hot line . . . unless you have one of those lunch cards. They don't take them here."

Terence's skin goes cold. *He* has one of those prepaid lunch cards. Somehow his dad actually remembered to sign him up for one before he started at Franklin, and it's got all his lunch money on it.

Eddie catches on quick, and her mouth falls open. She covers it with one hand. "Oh! I'm sorry."

Terence shakes his head and smiles. "It's fine," he says, struggling to remember if there's any actual money in his wallet today. "I do have a card, but I have some cash too. I mean, I can buy something. Probably."

Eddie sighs, like it's a huge relief, and scampers up to the bagel counter. "Plain with cream cheese and an extra cream cheese."

"That's fifty—" the man behind the counter starts.

Eddie cuts him off. "Fifty cents extra, I know, I know," she says, and then glances at Terence over her shoulder. "What are you having?"

"Same as you, I guess?" he says.

Eddie orders another and pulls folded bills from the front pocket of her jeans. "It's on me."

"No, really," Terence begins to object, hurrying to the cash register.

Eddie blocks him with her body. "Really, it's the least I could do, Weird Terry."

"What, because you won't join my band?"

"Join?" Eddie says, laying her bills on the stainless counter. The cashier scoops them up and sucks her teeth as she counts. "You mean *found*. That's the word when you start a band with someone."

"Fine, *found* then."

"First of all, who said I'm not going to found a band with you?" Eddie says, putting out her hand for the change. "Second of all, that's not why it's the least I can do."

"Then why?" Terence says.

Eddie pockets her change and hands Terence a paper tray with a bagel and two little covered cups of cream cheese. He can see at once why she asked for an extra. They're tiny.

"Did you ever wonder," Eddie says as she leaves the snack bar, Terence hurrying along behind her, "why I was in the office the other morning?"

"Actually, yes," Terence says. "I figured you were in trouble for something?"

She drops an icy glare before taking a seat at the end of a crowded table. Terence sits across from her, next to a boy he recognizes from his math class.

Or maybe science.

"I wasn't in trouble," Eddie says. "I don't *get* in trouble."

"You don't?" Terence says, squeaking in surprise.

"Is that so shocking?"

"Well, with the way you dress and . . . ," Terence stops, and then adds, "and your hair."

"Oh, please," Eddie says. "I'm unique, not criminal. In fact, I'm such a good student and so popular with the teachers and the principal that they chose *me* to meet the new student and show him around."

"What?" Terence says, loud enough so the other kids at the table look over at him.

Eddie laughs.

"What?" Terence repeats, whispering this time. "You were *supposed* to be helping me?"

She shrugs. "Yeah, and in fact way more than I did. I was supposed to hook up with you at lunch, help you find your way, even make sure you got to the bus — or the *late* bus — on time. Maybe I should have warned you about locking up your bike in the wrong place too."

Terence leans back in his chair. "I can't believe this."

"I know," Eddie says, nodding. "But look. We didn't exactly hit it off. I figured we'd both be better off if I just left you alone."

Terence thinks back to his confiscated bike, the rainstorm, and the late bus he didn't even know existed this time two days ago. "You were wrong."

"I know," Eddie says again. "I'm sorry."

Terence picks up his bagel. "I need a knife."

"Are you threatening me?"

"No, to spread the cream cheese," Terence says.

Eddie shakes her head. "Like this." She tears off a chunk of her bagel, rips open the top of one of her cream cheese cups, and dips the chunk of bagel. "See?"

Terence copies her and pops a big chunk of bagel into his mouth. "At least there's one thing here better than at Hart," he says as he chews. "Lunch was awful. My mom made me bag lunch every day."

"Just the food?" Eddie says. "What about me?"

Terence shrugs and smiles, but he thinks about Polly Winger back at Hart, and about Simon and Jalen — the old band. *His* old band. "I guess you should probably audition," he finally says.

Eddie gives him a shocked look. "Didn't you hear me sing already?"

"Yeah, but I mean," Terence says, "the acoustics in the basement are pretty crazy. The reverb can be very . . . forgiving."

"Oh, please," Eddie says, tearing a piece of her bagel like she's tearing his head off. "Anyway, you have a lot of other people lining up to *found* this band with you?"

"Sure," Terence says. "You're not the only person I've met here, you know."

"Ha!" Eddie says. "Name one other."

Terence scrambles through his mind, struggling to recall the name of even one classmate, but he's too slow.

"See?" Eddie says.

"Still," Terence says. "You should audition. Can you meet me in the orchestra room before jazz band later?"

Eddie looks down at her bagel and seems to shrink into her chair. "Fine," she says quietly. "But if anyone else shows up, I'm not doing it."

Terence almost laughs. "You're scared to sing in front of people?"

"So?" Eddie says, looking up at him.

"Nothing," he says. "Lots of people get stage fright. It's just funny because you sing in the hall every day."

"I didn't know anyone was listening," Eddie says shyly.

Terence sits for a beat, looking at the girl across from him. She's easily six inches taller than him, dressed like she couldn't care less what anyone thinks, and has an amazing singing voice. But performing scares her. Might make the battle of the bands a little trickier.

"Anyway," he finally says. "We should have a few minutes. Enough for one song."

And just like that, her shy moment passes. She sits up straight, excited. "What songs do you know?"

"Lots of songs," Terence says. "I have a whole set list from my band back home — I mean, back at Hart."

"I know everything the jazz band has done for the last three years," she says. "My twin brother, Luke, joined in sixth grade, and I steal his sheet music."

"The big guy who plays sax?" Terence says.

Eddie nods as she pops the last of her bagel into her mouth.

"You got all the talent in the family?" Terence asks before he can stop himself, and feels his face go red.

Eddie smiles at him as she pushes her chair back. "He's not very good, is he?" she admits. "Anyway, see if you can sneak out of last hour a little early," she adds. "To make sure we have time."

"Sure," Terence says, watching her leave, though he has no idea how to sneak out early.

It's 3:25 that afternoon, and Ms. Holyoake is lecturing about different economic systems and the formation of the European Union. School ends in fifteen minutes, and five minutes after that the whole jazz band will turn up for practice.

It's now or never. Terence puts up his hand.

"Yes . . . ?" Ms. H struggles to remember his name.

Terence decides this isn't the best time to remind her. "Can I go to the bathroom?"

Ms. H glances at the clock over the whiteboard. "Can't it wait fifteen minutes?"

Terence opens his mouth to answer but instead just shakes his head. A few snickers crackle in the back of the room, but Terence ignores them.

"Fine, fine, go," Ms. H says, and immediately goes back to her lecture, her colored marker streaking across the whiteboard as she stands with her back to the class.

It's the perfect opportunity. Terence grabs his backpack as secretly as he can and quietly hurries from the room. All he can do is hope none of his classmates will tell Ms. H he took his stuff with him, which means he's obviously not coming back.

The halls are quiet and empty, but Terence knows monitors and security are roaming too — someplace. This is public school, after all. He moves through the corridors like a spy or a ninja, stopping at every corner and peeking carefully around, until he reaches the ramp to the basement and hurries down.

Terence hears her before he sees her. Though he notices she's singing a bit more quietly this afternoon, her voice is unmistakable as she coos the chilling refrain of "Now At Last," made famous by Blossom Dearie. He can tell it's not her typical range or style, but she still sounds good.

Terence stops around the corner from the band room, listening and waiting for her to finish. When she's done, he waits a bit more, and then jogs into view.

"Made it," he says, feigning breathlessness. "How much time do we have?"

"Plenty," Eddie says, crossing her arms, "and I know you were listening around the corner."

"How do you know?" Terence says.

"The light was behind you, genius," she says. "And you have a shadow."

Terence looks down, as if to catch the offending shade in the act. "Oh."

"Yeah, oh," she says, grabbing the band room door handle. "Come on."

They're alone. Mr. Bonk's office is dark, the door closed. Terence goes to the piano and plays the opening riff to "Now At Last."

Eddie rolls her eyes. "You just *heard* that."

"I wanna hear it again," Terence says, smiling. He nods at her as he reaches the vocals entrance, and through a little laughter, Eddie sings.

Polly Winger was a Blossom Dearie fan. Still is, Terence imagines. But when she sang "Now At Last," she never quite found the song's bittersweet romance. That's why Terence never put the song on the playlist. They stuck with the "fun" Blossom numbers, like "True to You In My Fashion" and "Rhode Island Is Famous for You."

But Eddie nails it. Her voice is light and airy, and even in the ironically poor acoustics of the band room, it sounds full and bright. Terence forces himself to watch the keys as he plays, because though he knows the part well, he doesn't want Eddie to catch him staring at her.

It's a short song, and they slow down together as Eddie sings the last line: *"Now at last, I know."*

Eddie immediately covers her face with her hands.

"That was really good," Terence says quickly.

"Thanks," she says, her voice muffled by her hands. "I know my voice isn't right for Blossom Dearie songs, but—"

"No, it's great," Terence interrupts. "You don't sound like her, but that doesn't matter."

"Really?"

Terence looks back at the piano keys. "Should we do one more?" he says. "We have time."

Eddie bites her lip and nods once.

Terence thinks a minute, and then launches into something completely different. Laughing, Eddie joins in on vocals, and when Mr. Bonk comes in a couple of minutes later, they're knee-deep in a ridiculous cover of Bruno Mars's "Uptown Funk."

Eddie stops singing immediately, but Terence plays on. Mr. Bonk grins and even dances a little as he walks past to unlock his office. "Finish up!" he calls over his shoulder as he disappears inside.

"That was embarrassing," Eddie says, sitting next to Terence on the bench.

Terence slides over a little to make more room. "Nah, he didn't care," he says. "He probably wishes you'd join the jazz band."

"The jazz band doesn't have a vocalist," Eddie points out.

"Not *yet*," Terence says, but sitting this close to her is making his palms sweat, so he leans back like he's stretching, hops up from the bench, and hurries into Mr. Bonk's office.

"Um, Terence?" she calls after him.

He sticks his head out the door. "Great job. I have to get ready for jazz band now."

"Did I pass the audition?" Eddie says, still sitting at the piano.

"Oh," Terence says. "I'll, um, let you know. Bye!"

And with that, he grabs his bass from the storage area in Bonk's office and waits until he's sure Eddie has left.

CHAPTER FIVE

This is new.

Terence wakes the next morning having dreamed about Eddie: Eddie singing, Eddie laughing, Eddie leading him through the halls of Franklin Middle, Eddie shouting at him angrily and him shouting back.

Of course then he starts crying, and his mom shows up and it's an ordinary dream again, the kind he's been having for the last six months.

"Dad," Terence says, standing at his father's bedside, shaking the man by the shoulders. "Wake up. I need a ride this morning."

Dad rolls over and sits up groggily. He rubs his eyes

and gently grabs Terence by the wrist. "What's up? I was up too late again."

"Doing what?" Terence asks, pulling his arm away.

Dad shrugs and stretches and yawns. "Avoiding the bed." He throws his legs over the side of the bed and grabs the bunched-up jeans from the floor. "Give me two minutes, OK?"

Terence nods and heads out to the kitchen. He's eaten already, and he's dressed and ready to go, so he sits at the little table-for-two, puts on his headphones, and brings up the playlist he created last year for Polly. The first song is "It Don't Mean a Thing."

Two minutes in, while Ella Fitzgerald is scatting up a storm, Terence is leaning back in the chair, his face pointed toward the ceiling and his eyes closed, when Dad grabs his shoulder and gives him a shake. The headphones slip from his head and fall to the floor.

"Come on," Dad says. "I've been calling you."

"Sorry." Terence scoops up his headphones and follows Dad out the front door to the car, the only thing that proves for sure they used to be comfortable, happy, a family. It's Mom's car: a long, burgundy red, four-door sedan with heated front seats and a quality sound system. Mom was always the one who cared about music.

"What happened to your bike again?" Dad says

through a yawn. He sits too close to the steering wheel, leaning over it a little, as if he still can't quite see through the haze of sleep. Of course, he's been under a haze of sleep for months now.

"'Confiscated,'" Terence says. "I didn't know where I was supposed to chain it up."

"Will you get it back?"

Terence shrugs. "I'm trying."

Dad nods, briefly climbing out of his haze. "Let me know if I need to call the school."

Terence thinks about the man in the front office, who always seems to be on the phone with someone. It might be the way to reach him. But no; Terence doesn't need his dad involved.

"I'll take care of it."

Dad pulls up to the curb in front of Franklin Middle and glances at the dashboard clock. "Why are you here so early?"

Terence doesn't say that he can't bear to ride the bus because only one face doesn't make him want to run and hide under his blankets. But it's the one face he truly gets sick about seeing, especially after dreaming about that face half the night.

"Gonna try to get my bike back," Terence says as he climbs out of the car. Before Dad can reply, Terence slams the door and hurries inside.

The cafeteria is serving free breakfast, and Terence can smell the pancakes and syrup and turkey sausage. The sounds of students eating echo in the empty hallways.

The office is open too and bubbling with activity, at least compared to how Terence has seen it so far. The man is there, way back from the counter, but his headset isn't on yet. Teachers of all grades and subjects — including Ms. Hardison, his first-hour teacher — mill around near the mailboxes, sipping coffee from cardboard cups and chipped novelty mugs.

Terence moves invisibly past them and right up to the counter. He leans over and says in the loudest, most confident voice he can muster, "Excuse me. How do I get my bike back?"

The man looks up. So do most of the faculty standing around him.

"Terence Kato, right?" the man says, turning his eyes to the computer display in front of him. He types a bit.

"Yes."

The man spends a minute reading the display. "Ah, here it is," the man says. "Students aren't permitted to lock up bicycles in front of the school. Ample bicycle parking is made available on the north and south walkways."

"I didn't know."

"Your student handbook states the rules very clearly, Mr. Kato," the man says, typing a bit more.

"Oh help him out, Sam," says Ms. Hardison leaning on the counter next to Terence and actually winking at him. She smells like shampoo and espresso. "He's new, and he's been through enough."

What does she know about what I've been through? Terence thinks, and then it occurs to him that she — and much of the faculty — might know quite a lot about what he's been through. They probably put stuff like that in student files.

Terence swallows and hard and scratches at a bit of dry ink on the counter.

Sam — the man at the desk — sighs and smirks and glares at Terence a minute. "You're new, so I'll give you a break — and a tip," he says. "Read your handbook. I don't want to see you in here again tomorrow because your iPod and headphones have been confiscated."

Note to self, Terence thinks. *No headphones.* Which is too bad, since the headphones now in his book bag are a major component of Operation: Avoid Talking to Eddie Because She Makes My Stomach Flip.

"I didn't know we had a handbook," Terence says.

"It was sent to your school email address when you registered," Sam says, crossing his arms and cocking his eyebrows.

"I didn't know I had a school email address," Terence says. "How do I access it?"

"Those instructions are in your handbook," Sam says.

"But how can I read the handbook if I can't . . . ," Terence says, but the rest of his obvious question is drowned out by the first bell.

Sam rises from his seat and presents Terence with a pink form: "Confiscated item requisition form S14-A." Boxes, lines, and tiny print cover the form.

"Fill this out," Sam says, slapping a pen on the counter. "You can pick up your bike from the equipment shed on the south end of the athletic field at end of classes. Don't make me wait."

"I won't," Terence says, and he grabs the pen and glances at Ms. Hardison. "Thanks."

She winks again, grabs some papers from her mailbox, and leaves.

With the form handed in and one of his major problems hopefully solved, Terence shoulders his book bag, keeps his head down, and hurries to Ms. Hardison's class for first hour.

He zips through the front hall, keeping his eyes down, desperately trying to stay invisible.

At least it's Friday, Terence tells himself. *Then I'll*

have the whole weekend to figure out how to deal with the Eddie problem.

At the bottom of the steps, though, he knocks into someone — an unfortunate side effect of keeping his head down.

"Watch it, weirdo," says a stomach-flip-inducing voice.

Terence looks up, right into Eddie's grinning face.

"You ran off pretty suddenly yesterday," she says.

"Oh, sorry," Terence says, averting his eyes and shuffling past her to the steps. "I better get going. Don't wanna be late."

"Hey!" she calls after him.

He glances back to see her standing at the bottom of the steps, one hand on the banister, blocking traffic, but he doesn't stop.

"I *know* my singing wasn't *that* bad!" she shouts.

Terence hurries from the stairwell, slumps into his desk, and tries to catch his breath.

"Glad you made it, Terence," Ms. Hardison says from the front of the room. "Did Sam end up helping you?"

"Um, yeah," Terence says. "I'll have my bike back this afternoon."

"Good." She smiles at him and begins the day's lesson. "Now, who can tell me the difference between *rational* and *irrational*?"

Terence slumps lower in his seat. This week has gone about as irrationally as one could.

CHAPTER SIX

At lunch, sitting in the crowded cafeteria, tucked away in a corner with his hood up and his head down, Terence manages to avoid Eddie's eye.

And while he's sitting there, surrounded by all these people he doesn't know, he gets an idea: among all these other kids, surely a few must love singing.

Surely a couple must be *great* singers.

Certainly at least one must be a good singer, who loves singing, and who won't turn up in Terence's dreams uninvited.

He takes a deep breath, leans closer to the stranger next to him — a boy in a polo shirt and khaki pants that even Terence knows are not in style — and says,

"Do you know anyone in this school who likes to sing?"

"Pardon?" the boy says. He has the slightest accent, like maybe he spent a summer in England and never quite got over it.

"Someone who loves to sing?" Terence says. "Someone who might like to join a band?"

"Oh, I don't sing," the boy says. "I'm a poet."

"No, I didn't mean you," Terence says, adding quickly, "necessarily. But does anyone in school sing?"

The boy looks around over the sea of faces. "Probably," he finally says, and goes back to eating his lunch.

"Thanks," Terence says. "Very helpful."

Still, once Eddie finishes her lunch and leaves, Terence hurries from table to table, asking if anyone knows anyone at all — in sixth, seventh, or eighth grade — who sings. He gets a few names, and meets a few people, and when the bell rings to end the hour, he feels a bit better, like maybe he won't be stuck in a band with Eddie.

In fact, he's almost smiling as he leaves the cafeteria, but the moment he steps into the hall, Eddie stops him with a stiff palm to his chest.

"Weirdo," she says, as if it's his name.

"Oh," Terence says. "Hi."

"Are you avoiding me?" she asks.

Terence shakes his head and sputters and spits.

"Are you?" she says again.

"How do you do that?" Terence finally says. "How do you just come out and say what you're thinking?"

"What else would I say?"

"I don't know," Terence admits. "Nothing. I'd say nothing."

"You're good at that," Eddie says, laughing a little.

"I have to get to my next class," Terence says, dropping his head and starting off.

But Eddie grabs his book bag and stops him. "Hold up," she says. "You've been asking literally everyone in school if they know any singers."

"How do you know that?" Terence asks.

She shrugs. "I guess people know I like to sing," she says, "so a few people mentioned it."

"Word travels fast."

"So?" she says, pointing her chin at him. "You don't want me in the band."

"It's not like that," Terence says, starting to walk off again.

Eddie hurries alongside. "Then what?" she says. "You need backup singers too?"

"No."

"Then what?"

Terence stops and glares at her. He retreats into a corner. "Look, I like the way you sing, OK?" he says quietly. "A lot."

"Thanks."

Terence looks at his sneakers. "And I like *you*," he says, quieter still, so she has to lean down a little to hear him, "a lot."

"So what's the problem?" Eddie says. "So we play music and have fun. We've got a band. Or a duo of friends, anyway. It's a good start."

"I don't *want* friends, Eddie," he says, finally looking into her eyes.

"Why not?" she asks. She really looks like she can't understand.

The truth is, Terence doesn't fully understand either, and when Eddie puts the question to him like that, he's forced to think about why for the first time.

"Because this school," he says slowly, his mind far away, "my time here, the band I want to put together . . . none of it's real."

"Um," she says, "I feel pretty real." She grabs her cheek and gives it a pinch. "Yup. Real."

"For you," Terence says. "But for me?" He thinks about his mom and her sickness and the months since, and it's all he can do not to cry in front of her, so he just shakes his head again.

Eddie's face falls. For the first time since he met her, it's not grinning or scowling or snarling. It's just sad.

"Sorry," he says.

Now Eddie is the one who can't speak. She shakes her head. "Let me join the band."

"Of course," he says. "Obviously you're in the band. I'm sorry for — for avoiding you, for hiding."

"I get it," she says. "You don't have to explain."

"Thanks."

Around them, the halls have emptied. Only a few voices and stray footsteps remain. "Now we really better get to class," Eddie says. "Mr. Amal is gonna kill me if I'm late for bio again."

She backs away, her eyes still on Terence.

"You OK?" she asks.

Terence nods and forces a smile.

"Good," she says as she skips away toward the science wing. "And don't worry about us being friends," she adds over her shoulder, that playful grin returning to her face. "I don't like you that much anyway."

Terence can't help laughing as Eddie disappears around the corner. He wipes at his eyes to make sure they're tear-free, and then turns the corner toward Language Arts class — and right into the broad chest and gritted teeth of one saxophone-playing brother named Luke.

"Sorry," Terence says.

Luke gives him a light shove — light but hard enough to knock Terence stumbling backward. "If you hurt my sister," Luke says, "I'll hurt you back."

"Hurt her?" Terence says, backing away a little more. "She's bigger than me!"

Luke snarls.

"Look, we're just going to play music together," Terence says, hands up and still backing away. "Nothing else going on here."

Luke growls and closes the gap between them.

"Really," Terence insists. "You have nothing to worry about."

Luke bears his teeth.

"And I'm going to be late for Language Arts!" Terence says. With that, he dodges to the right, runs past Luke, and takes off down the hall and into his classroom.

Terence drops into his desk at the back of the class and mutters to himself, "Life here is going to be interesting."

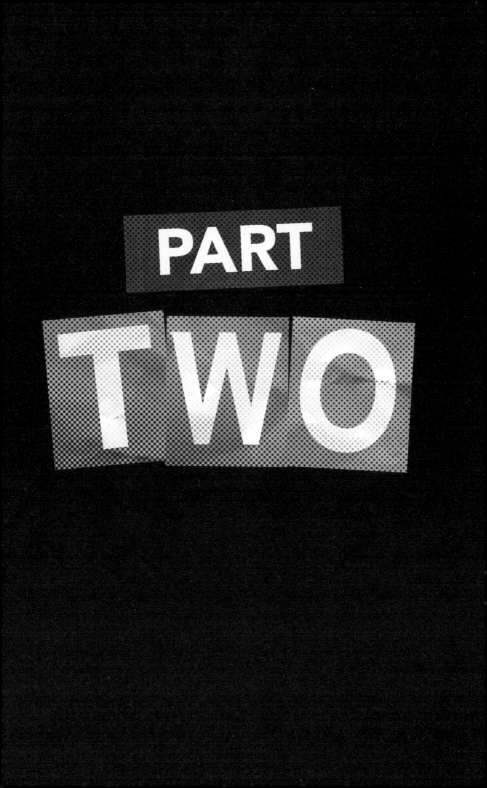

PART

TWO

CHAPTER SEVEN

It's Monday morning, and Terence founded his new band exactly sixty-seven and a half hours ago. Not that he's played, or practiced, or even spoken to Eddie since riding the bus home with her on Friday afternoon.

Terence hunches his shoulder against the January chill and shoves his hands deeper into the pockets of his hoodie. He wishes he had his gloves, or rather, he wishes he knew where his gloves were. But with the move from the old house to the rental, eighty percent of his stuff —and Dad's stuff — remains in boxes in the corner of their living room.

Neither he nor his dad relished the idea of opening any of those boxes, whatever the need, because what if they opened a box full of Mom's stuff? Terence doesn't think he can handle that. He *knows* Dad can't handle it.

Terence hears the bus before he sees it. Next comes a poof of thick gray smoke just before the front of the bus peeks over the hill on the next block. It seems to take forever to chug its way along. The brakes squeak and the doors open with an airy *thwack*, and Terence climbs aboard.

Eddie saved him a seat.

"Good morning, bandmate!" she says, sliding over for him and grinning madly. Eddie grins madly a lot, Terence has learned in his first week at Franklin Middle. In fact, she seems to do everything a little madly, including dress herself. Today she's wearing a black, white, and gray patched skirt over red jeans and a black Beatles T-shirt over a green thermal.

In her hands, she's got a black three-ring binder, decorated with puffy stickers and drawings and scribblings in Wite-Out. The biggest one — right in the middle, in thick cursive — says "Songs."

"Hi," Terence says. "Um . . . what's that?"

She pats the cover affectionately. "This is my song book," she says. "I don't know when we'll get to play again, but I thought I could show you some of these."

"Sure," Terence says slowly. "I mean, I'd like to hear them. Do you play guitar too?"

She shakes her head. "Well, a little," she says. "I'm just good enough to play some chords to back myself, you know? Just to write the melodies." She slumps in her seat in a little. "I'm so relieved. I thought you would think it was silly."

"Songwriting, silly?" Terence says. "Of course not. Why would I think that? It's great that you write songs. Someday you can form your own band and perform them, when you're ready."

"Wait, what?" she says.

Terence straightens in his seat and looks at the back of the seat in front of them. "I just mean, you know, this is *my* band."

"Oh, is it?"

He nods. "I have a set list all planned, is the thing," Terence says. "It's the same one we played in my old band."

"At the private school."

"At Hart, yeah," Terence says. "If those songs were good enough for the virtuosos at Hart, they'll be good enough for you, right?"

Eddie's smile falls away for an instant, but then she's right back to grinning, her lip-glossed mouth stretched into madness. "Right," she says, slipping her binder back into her bag.

"So I was thinking," Terence says, "I can play piano

for practicing a little, but I'm better on bass, and I prefer it, so we should find a keys player right away."

Eddie stares out the window as the bus rolls along Riverside Drive.

"Eddie?" Terence says.

"What?" she says. "Oh, a piano player. Right. For sure."

"Do you know anyone who plays?" Terence asks.

"Just you," she says.

Terence smirks.

"I'll ask Luke," Eddie says.

"Um, I don't know if that's a good idea," Terence says, twisting in his seat to check out her brother sitting at the back of the bus with his big, scary friends. They're all acting crazy, swinging on the seats, shouting and throwing pencils at each other.

Except Luke. He's just sitting in the aisle seat and staring — at Terence.

"I think he's going to eat me," Terence says, straightening in his seat again.

"Oh, stop," Eddie says. "He's just . . . confused. You're weird."

"Right, I keep forgetting."

"Anyway, he's been playing sax since second grade," Eddie says. "Even if he's not very good. He's bound to know someone who plays piano after all those years."

"If you say so," Terence says. The bus pulls up to the curb in front of Franklin Middle. "Listen, I'm quitting jazz band."

"What?" Eddie says as they shuffle down the bus aisle to climb off. "Bonk's going to cry."

"Doubt it," Terence says. "He doesn't like my improvisational style anyway."

A few teachers are holding the doors open as the buses arrive, like every day, and Terence and Eddie mumble good-mornings and accept flaccid high fives.

"Besides," Terence continues, following Eddie to her locker, "if I have after-school stuff every day, when will we ever practice?"

"It's your life," Eddie says as she opens her locker and drops off her book bag, save a notebook and textbook, which she shoves under one arm. She slams the locker. "See you at lunch?"

"Sure," Terence says, and Eddie skips down the hall.

Terence turns to head to his advisory class — and walks right into the ample, wall-like chest of Luke.

"Watch it," Luke says.

"Sorry," Terence says, moving to go around the cinderblock wall of a boy.

Luke grabs his arm. "You better be nice to her."

"I will!" Terence says, struggling to free himself from Luke's grip. "I mean, I am!"

Luke releases him, grunts menacingly, and stomps off.

"Great," Terence mutters to himself and he plods toward advisory. "That guy's our primary source for a keys player. This ought to be good."

"You talkin' to yourself, weirdo?"

Terence looks up and finds a pair of boys as big as Luke, and twice as mean looking. They stand shoulder to shoulder, blocking his path.

"Hey, you're that new kid," says the uglier one. His nose looks like he might have played pro hockey in a previous life. "The one from Hart Arts and Farts."

"I just want to get to class," Terence says, keeping his eyes on the floor.

"Oh, you're not going to class," says the bully on the left, grinning down at Terence. He reaches out slowly, takes Terence by the front of his shirt, and lifts him off the ground.

The other bully steps around behind him and snatches his book bag.

"Come on!" Terence protests as the first boy drops him. Together, they open his bag and dump the contents all over the floor. At the same moment, the late bell rings.

The two bullies stand over Terence as he crouches to pick up his stuff.

"We're just gonna dump it again," says one.

But just then, high heels click and clack around the corner. Principal Stone appears and puts her hands on her hips.

"Aren't you two going to help him pick up his things?" she says.

The bullies almost seem like they will, but Terence quickly shoves the books and papers and pens back into his bag and rises. "I'm fine, Ms. Stone," he says.

"Good," she says with an icy glare. "Now get to class, all of you."

The bullies hurry off. Principal Stone puts a hand on Terence's shoulder before he can scamper off. "And no more tardiness, either. You're new, but by now you ought to know what time class starts, OK?"

"Sorry," Terence says, hurrying away.

CHAPTER EIGHT

Unlike back at Hart Arts — a school whose focus was strictly on the arts and where the core curriculum of math, science, history, and language took a backseat — here at Franklin Middle the arts are completely ignored.

Sure, there are drawing electives and the after-school jazz band. But the classes — the hours every student put in between 7:30 and 2:30, aside from lunch — were all core curriculum. Back at Hart, Terence might have spent the whole morning in a little sealed room with three other students, a piano, a double bass, maybe a couple horns.

The negatives of this change for someone like Terence are obvious. But there are positives too. This morning, the main positive is that Terence moves from class to class, seeing nearly every student in eighth grade.

"Hi," Terence says to the boy at the next desk as he takes his seat in the back of Mr. Ellison's social studies class.

"Um," the boy says, looking around a little, "hi?"

"I'm new," Terence says.

"I know."

"I was wondering," Terence says, "do you know anyone who plays piano?"

The boy stares at him blankly for a long moment before finally saying, his face contorted in confusion, "I don't think so. Do we need a piano player in social studies class?"

"No," Terence says. "Not usually."

"Oh, good," the boy says, settling into his seat and facing the teacher at the front of the class.

Terence takes part in several equally awkward conversations throughout his day. In study hall — which students are forced to spend in one lecture hall in relative silence, compared to study hall at Hart when Terence would would have spent the time in a practice space jamming with Polly and the others — Terence leans along the aisle of the lecture hall.

"Hey," he whispers to a nearby girl.

The girl looks at him briefly. "Hi," she says, smiling. "Hey, you're the new boy. The weird one, right?"

Terence almost rolls his eyes, but she's smiling at him, and he thinks he recognizes her as a girl in his first-hour math class. "Some people think so."

The girl twists her neck to look back at Mr. Ghoti, the study-hall monitor. Then she grabs her book bag and purse from the seat between them and hops into the seat to be next to Terence.

"So what's your *story*?" she says, leaning on the armrest between them. "Where'd you come from? Aliana says you moved here from Russia, but that's obviously not true."

She leans a little closer.

"Right?"

Terence leans back and checks to make sure Mr. Ghoti is still distracted by the magazine he's reading.

"Um, right," Terence says. "I'm definitely not from Russia. Actually, I've always lived around here. We just moved from across town." He swallows and adds even more quietly, "And I had to change schools."

"Tell me everything about your old school," the girl says. "Was it as horrible as this place?"

Terence thinks about Hart Arts — his friends there, his band, the music, the relaxed atmosphere, hallways full of singing. But he doesn't say any of this.

"Actually," Terence says, straightening in his seat, "I was just wondering if you know anyone who plays piano."

She stares back at him, her mouth hanging open.

"Sorry, I just . . . ," Terence says, stammering a little, "I just don't feel like chatting right now." *Especially about Hart.*

"OK," she says, flinching as if he slapped her. Her voice now is icy and cracks like the top of a frozen puddle when you step on it. "No need to be rude."

"No, it's nothing like that," Terence says as she hops back into her original seat, stuffing her book bag between them again. "It's just that I'm not super interested in making friends here."

She glances at him as she opens a textbook in her lap and then puts her eyes on a random page.

"At Franklin, I mean," he says.

"Mmhm," she says, not looking up. "Not chatting."

"Right," Terence says. "But, um . . . do you? Know anyone?"

She slams her book closed and glares at him. "Melody Ulrich," she says, frigid, and then raises one finger and points to a girl at the bottom of the lecture hall. "Her."

Melody sits alone in the front row. She wears earbuds, has a notebook in her lap, a textbook open on the seat on her left and another on the right.

"Thanks," Terence says, and he gathers his stuff and makes his careful way along the aisle.

"Melody?" Terence says, sliding into the seat behind the girl.

She doesn't reply.

Terence taps her on the shoulder and she jumps and turns around. "What?" she snaps, pulling an earbud out.

"Sorry," Terence says. "Are you Melody?"

"So?" she says.

"Well," Terence says, getting nervous now as Melody seems to get more angry, "I hear you play piano."

"Are you trying to be funny?" Melody says.

Terence thinks for a second. "Am I being funny?"

Melody rolls her eyes. "Yes, I play piano. I've been playing piano since I was three years old. Everyone knows I play piano, OK?"

"OK."

"What are you, new here or something?" Melody says, pushing her earbud back in.

"Yes, actually," Terence says, kind of pleased that someone in his class at Franklin *doesn't* know he's the new, weird kid.

Of course Melody doesn't hear him, since her earbud is back in. But Terence hasn't even had a chance to mention the band yet. He taps her shoulder again.

"What?" she snaps, again tugging her earbud out.

"I'm starting a band," Terence says.

"Good for you."

"And we need a piano player," Terence adds.

Her face softens a bit. "Oh," she says. "You want *me*?"

Terence shrugs a little. He was sure he at least wanted to hear her play a few minutes ago, but now . . . "I was hoping you'd audition."

She closes the book on her lap and pulls out her other earbud. "I don't need to audition."

"You don't?"

She shakes her head. "I'm the best pianist at Franklin, probably better than the ham-fisted players at the high school too."

"Still," Terence says. "I should probably hear you play."

The bell to end study hall rings, and Melody starts packing up her books as she stands. "Suit yourself," she says. "Come to my house this afternoon. I have a fifteen-minute window at 4:30, after my Latin tutor and before my krav maga class."

"Krav ma—?" Terence starts to say. "Sure. 4:30. Can do."

"Give me your phone."

Terence obeys, and Melody quickly types in her number and address. "See you."

With that, she hurries off to her next class.

Terence gathers his stuff and leaves the lecture hall.

"Hey, Weird Terry." It's Eddie, waiting just outside the lecture hall, ready to pounce. "Tell me you didn't just ask Melody Ulrich to join our band."

"I might have," Terence says slowly. "Why?"

Eddie sighs. "Look, forget about her," she says. "Luke's friend Claude can do it."

"Luke's friend?" Terence says. "I don't know...." He looks over Eddie's shoulder. Luke is there, a little way down the hall and in close conversation with another big guy who must be Claude.

Claude is a little taller than Luke, and broader too. He's wearing black jeans, big black boots, and a black denim jacket open to reveal a ragged-looking white T-shirt bearing a grinning skull. His black (of course) hair is long and greasy looking.

"Him?"

Eddie glances and waves. The boys don't wave back. "Him," Eddie says.

"Look, let's just hear Melody play," Terence says. Terence can probably get used to having Luke around now and then, but a boy even bigger than Luke, twice as scary, and playing keys for *his band*? No way, especially after his run-in with Tweedledum and Tweedledee before advisory this morning.

Those two sure seemed like the kind of guys Luke hangs out with.

"I've heard Melody play," Eddie says with a straight face. "She's amazing."

Terence cocks his head. "OK then," he says. "Then she's the one for us, right?"

"I didn't say that."

The bell rings, sending kids all around hurrying to their next classes. "Look, I'm going to hear her play at her house today. You should come."

"I told you," Eddie says as Terence backs away, anxious about being late to class. "I've heard her."

"Come anyway?" Terence says.

He hurries away, Eddie calling after him, "Fine! But it's a waste of time!"

Not long ago, if Terence Kato needed to get to a friend's house clear across the neighborhood — especially on a windy, snowy winter night — Terence would have asked his father for a ride.

It's funny. Even then, Mom wouldn't have been around, not by four in the afternoon, anyway. She'd be working, if she was even in town. Even so, things happened. Dad got things done. He gave Terence rides when he needed them, made dinner, cleaned up the house.

At 4:30 this afternoon though, with the snow picking up and the sun setting, Terence stops his bike in front of Melody Ulrich's house on the other side of his neighborhood.

He didn't even ask Dad for a ride. He barely stopped at home long enough to get his bike and put on his cold-weather face mask.

As he locks up his bike, a silver SUV pulls up, exhaust puffing from its tailpipes like Terence's breath as he biked over. Eddie hops out of the front seat, says something quickly to the driver, and hurries to Terence's side.

"You biked?" she says, hollering over the wind. "Are you insane?"

"My dad wasn't around," Terence says. It's not true.

"Come on!" Eddie jogs up the walk and rings the bell.

Melody pulls the door open instantly. "You biked?" she says to Terence, her brow knitted and her mouth twisted in derision.

"Yeah, my dad—" Terence starts to say, but Melody isn't listening.

"What is *she* doing here?" she asks, glaring at Eddie.

Eddie grins. "I'm the singer."

"The singer?" Melody says with disdain. She rolls her eyes as if to say *whatever*. "Follow me." She leads her guests along the front hall to a set of steps down to a cavernous basement.

It's set up like a recording studio, with a soundproof booth at the far end behind glass. Inside are mic stands, music stands, and a gleaming black grand piano.

"Wow," Terence says.

Eddie nods, her mouth open, speechless.

"Sit there," Melody says, gesturing briefly toward a slim and stylish couch along one wall, and she goes into the soundproof room.

Then she begins to play. The sound fills the room from speakers in the corners and woofers set into the walls near the floor.

"Chopin's Sonata no. 3 in B Minor," Terence whispers to Eddie.

She doesn't seem to care, but Melody's playing is flawless, and for the next twenty-five minutes Terence and Eddie sit silently and listen and watch her fingers dancing across the keys, her body swaying with the music, her eyes closed like she's mid-epiphany.

When she's done, Terence waits for the last chord to fade after the furious finish and jumps to his feet, applauding.

"That was amazing!" Terence says, hurrying to the booth's door as Melody comes out, actually smiling and reddening a little in the face.

"*Merci,*" Melody says, miming a little curtsey.

"I have to ask, though," Terence says, though it almost hurts to go on, "why aren't you enrolled at Hart? You'd probably get a full scholarship."

Melody's smile is gone. "Hart Arts?" she says, and quickly shakes her head, dismissive. "Zero focus on core curriculum. No thank you."

"No thank you?" Terence says, following Melody out of the studio. "But you're a genius at piano. Who needs math, right?"

"I'm no fool," she says as she stops in a basement kitchenette and pulls a bottled water from the little fridge. She leans on the counter as she drinks half the bottle. "Piano is no way to make a living. I intend to go to medical school."

"Wow," Terence says, leaning in the doorway. "What a waste."

"Anyway, you've heard enough, I assume?" Melody says.

"I mean, yeah," Terence says. "You're amazing. Do you know any Cole Porter? Duke Ellington? Lennon/McCartney?"

Melody sets down the bottle and laughs. "I learned 'Yesterday' when I was five," she says. "I can probably muddle through."

Muddle through? Terence things. "What about jazz?"

"I'm not so interested in jazz," Melody says.

"Rock?" Terence says. "Pop? Soul? R & B?"

"No," Melody says. "No, no, and no."

"You only play classical?" Terence asks as Eddie joins them in the kitchenette. "I don't understand."

"What's not to understand?" Eddie says. "I told you this was a waste of time. Melody Ulrich is a renowned snob at Franklin. Princess Melody since kindergarten."

Melody sneers at her.

"But why did you ask me to come down and listen," Terence says, "if you're not interested in joining a band anyway?"

"Well," Melody says, ushering the two of them out of the kitchenette and toward the stairs up to the first floor, "I didn't love the idea of a kid at Franklin not knowing what a piano genius I am."

"You've got to be kidding me," Terence says, letting Melody hurry them toward the door.

When she pulls it open, the wind and snow rush in and slap Terence in the face. He and Eddie step outside.

"Now I know, I guess!" Terence shouts over the furious weather.

Melody just smiles as she closes the door in their faces.

Eddie turns to him and slowly smiles, like that cat from *Alice in Wonderland*.

"Don't say it," Terence says.

"Don't say what?" Eddie says, feigning confusion.

"'I told you so,'" Terence says.

"I wouldn't dream of it."

The SUV at the curb toots its horn.

"Hey, do you want a ride?" Eddie asks. "It's pretty nasty out."

Terence glances at the SUV and then at his bike, chained to the street sign at the corner. A ride would be good; a conversation with a mom and this *thing* with Eddie actually turning into friendship would not.

"I'll be OK," Terence says. "I like winter biking." Actually he hates it.

"Suit yourself," Eddie says. "See you tomorrow. We can tell Claude he's in the band."

"No way!"

Eddie sticks out her tongue and jogs to the car, and a moment later it pulls away from the curb and vanishes into the darkening afternoon, a cloud of exhaust lingering at the curb in its place.

"Whoever heard of a big, dumb muscle-brain playing piano anyway?" Terence mutters to himself as he climbs onto his bike.

The ride home is tough, cold, and miserable, and when he gets there Dad's on the couch with a bag of sour-cream-and-onion chips and *The A-Team* streaming on TV.

Terence crosses in front of the TV and only says, "I'll be in my room."

CHAPTER NINE

Over the next few days, Terence manages to put off recruiting a pianist despite Eddie and Luke bringing up Claude at every opportunity.

"There must be someone else," Terence says, and, "Have we talked to the kids in seventh grade? Sixth?"

"Maybe we can recruit someone out of the elementary school," Eddie jokes, crossing her arms and narrowing her eyes.

"Maybe . . . ," Terence hems.

"Come over after school," Eddie says on Friday morning as they climb off the bus in front of the school. "We can practice."

"Just us?" Terence asks.

Eddie shrugs. "Sure," she says. "Unless you found someone to play keys."

Terence shakes his head.

"OK then," Eddie says, scurrying off to her first class. "You can play my guitar while I sing!"

By four o'clock, Terence sits on a folding chair in Eddie's family room, her acoustic guitar in his lap. "Now, I'm not great at guitar," he explains as he tunes. "I can't play pop standards."

"What *do* you know on guitar?" Eddie asks.

"Beatles?" Terence says, quietly strumming with his thumb. "A couple of Paul Simon songs. Um, I know one Suzanne Vega song."

"Who?"

"Never mind," Terence says, and then adds quickly, "Oh, and some Nirvana."

Eddie frowns at him and shakes her head. "Play a Beatles song."

He thinks a moment. "'With a Little Help From My Friends?'"

Eddie nods, pleased. "Play it slowly, like the Joe Cocker version."

Terence strums the opening E chords, choppy at first like the Beatles did it, and then slows into a mellow, relaxed strum.

Eddie picks up the rhythm, tapping her foot and nodding in time, and then starts singing.

She was right, Terence decides; the Cocker version is definitely more her style than the original would have been. She has a little of Cocker's growl, but her voice is rich and smoky, not nearly as erratic and wild as his was.

Halfway through, she's really belting it out, and Luke comes and leans in the family room doorway, watching them. It's a short song, and Eddie doesn't vamp the ending. She just stops when it's over and looks over at Luke.

"Well?" she says.

"That was good," he says, and then looks at Terence and adds, "Not that you contribute much."

"Thanks," Terence says.

Luke shrugs and exits.

"We can do that one, right?" Eddie says, scooting forward on the couch. "That was fun."

"Yeah, I think so," Terence says. "Your singing style would be enough to make it fit in the set I have in mind."

"Cool," Eddie says. "Maybe you're not a complete dictator after all."

"What?" Terence says. *Dictator?*

"Nothing, nothing," Eddie says. "Do another one."

Terence looks at her a minute, but she just smiles

back at him. He picks out a few notes, refreshing his memory, and starts playing "Bridge Over Troubled Water."

After a few more songs, Terence leans the guitar against the front of the couch. "I should probably head home," he says.

Eddie rises to walk him to the door. "We sound pretty good."

"*You* sound pretty good," Terence says.

Eddie grins and hits him on the arm. "Can we play more tomorrow?"

"My place," Terence says. "I prefer accompanying you on piano, and I have an electric keyboard in my room."

"Cool," Eddie says. "Around lunchtime?"

Terence thinks: will he be able to get his dad out of bed by then? Dressed, even? Maybe even out of the house? "Sure," he says. "Noon."

When he gets home, he sneaks into Dad's room and sets the alarm for 9:30, just to be on the safe side.

CHAPTER TEN

It's 9:32 when Dad plods out of his bedroom the next morning, wrapped in his robe over baby-blue pajama pants. "Are we doing something today?"

"Nope," Terence says, feigning innocence. "Why do you ask?"

"My alarm went off," Dad says, dropping into a kitchen chair and yawning like a bear on the first of spring. "I haven't used that thing in months."

"I don't know," Terence says, and he places a big mug of coffee with cream in front of his dad. "My friend — I mean, a girl from school — is coming over today. We're starting a new band."

Dad's eyebrows rise as he takes a big sip of his coffee.

"Great," he says and then looks at the coffee as if seeing it for the first time. "Did you make this?"

Terence nods.

Dad makes an impressed face, takes another sip, and stretches. "Well," he says, lightly slapping the table with both hands, "I'm gonna get dressed."

"Yes," Terence whispers to himself.

Dad does get dressed, but by 11:59, he's in front of the TV, a bag of chips in his lap. When the doorbell rings, Terence sighs and opens the door.

"Hi," he says, miserable.

Eddie is, as usual, grinning. "Ready for me?"

Terence checks with Dad over his shoulder, but the old man didn't even hear the doorbell, or is so absorbed in marathoning *Star Trek: The Next Generation,* that he can't be bothered to look up.

"Sure," Terence says, closing the door. "Come on."

Terence cleaned up his room a bit in the morning, and he takes a seat at the little bench in front of his electric piano.

Eddie sits on the edge of the bed. There's really nowhere else to sit in Terence's little bedroom. He runs his fingers over the keys — it's set to organ, so he switches it to piano — and adjusts the volume.

"Any requests?"

Eddie leans forward so her head is right next to his

shoulder and looks at his hands on the keys. "What do you know?"

"On piano?" Terence says. "More like what do I *not* know."

"Why are we looking for a keys player again?" she asks.

Terence shakes his head. "I play bass. I love playing bass. I play bass."

"Suit yourself," she says. "Who ever heard of a bass-playing band leader?"

"Um, Jaco Pastorius?" Terence says, looking askew at her.

"Who?"

"Google him later," Terence says. He plays the opening lines of "Yesterday" by the Beatles. "How about Paul McCartney?"

"He wasn't the *leader*," Eddie argues.

"Fine," Terence says, sighing. "Gene Simmons then."

"From Kiss?" she asks. "Are you kidding?"

Terence shrugs as he finds the broken chords to open Kiss's classic "Beth."

"Stop," Eddie says. "My mother loves that song."

"Mine too." Terence bites his lip at the memory.

Eddie leans back. "You have to clean the aura in here now," she says. "Play Cole Porter or Gershwin or something, quick."

Terence manages a smile and starts in on "I Won't Dance."

"Jerome Kern," Eddie says, standing up. "That works." And after a beat, she launches into the song. After a couple of lines, she elbows Terence. "Take it!" she shouts.

Terence shakes his head. The song is a duet, strictly speaking, but Frank Sinatra and so many others recorded it alone. Eddie won't let up, so Terence — quietly — takes a verse, Eddie grinning at him the whole time.

His face goes red as he finishes the phrase, but he can't help smiling as he looks down at the keys and shakes his head again.

Eddie elbows him once more as she takes on the vocals, and when she finishes the song, she grabs his shoulder. "That was pretty good!"

"Nah," Terence says.

"Look, you're not Nat King Cole," she says, "but it wasn't bad."

"Gee, thanks," Terence says, crossing his arms.

Eddie shrugs, and a moment later Dad appears in the doorway, scowling a little. "Hey, turn the radio down a notch, OK? I can hardly hear the TV in there." With that, he walks away.

Eddie looks at Terence, her eyebrows up, and then bursts into laughter. Terence laughs too.

"He thought we were the radio!" Eddie says through her laughter, wiping her eyes. "That's pretty good!"

"But," Terence says, almost breathless, "I told him you were coming over to play music."

Eddie laughs even more, and Terence catches his breath.

"He wasn't even listening!" Terence says. "He's barely even here!"

That makes Eddie crack up, but just for a moment, because Terence isn't laughing anymore. He's slumped on the piano bench, shoulders drooping, hands folded on his lap.

"Hey, hey, Terry," Eddie says, putting a hand on his arm. "You OK?"

"Ever since Mom died, Dad is just . . . ," Terence starts, staring at his hands. "It's like he's just checked out."

Tears fill his eyes and, before he can bat them away, drop onto his hands like giant raindrops.

Eddie eases onto the bench beside him and puts an arm around his shoulders. "I didn't know," she says.

"I don't like to talk about it," he says, but he can't stop himself. "I miss her. So much."

Then he's bawling, sobbing, right there at the piano with this girl he barely knows sitting next to him, comforting him. He feels like such a fool, such a baby, and he pulls himself free and stands in the middle of the room.

"Please go now," he says, surprised at how angry his own voice sounds. "I told you I'm not looking for a friend."

"Terry—" she says, reaching for him.

"Go!" Terence snaps, and Eddie jumps up from the bench and hurries from the room. A moment later, he hears the front door slam.

Terence drops onto his bed and cries.

CHAPTER ELEVEN

Terence spends much of Sunday imitating Dad. He stays in bed as much as possible, watches sitcoms on the laptop in his room, and ignores a couple of text messages from Eddie.

Well, that last part isn't an imitation of Dad, obviously.

On Monday morning, Terence has been in and out of sleep for almost two solid days. He wakes up to the theme song to his favorite show, *The X-Files*, which has been marathoning on his laptop all night. That explains the dream he had about Mom and Agent Mulder skulking through a foggy forest with flashlights.

Terence sits up and closes the streaming tab in his

browser and sees a new email too. It's from Eddie, and an MP3 is attached. The only text in the email is "keys player — listen!"

Terence almost clicks the link, but instead he closes the laptop and rolls out of bed. "Dad!" he calls through the house. No answer.

Terence pulls on a pair of jeans from the back of his desk chair and goes into the hall. "Dad," he says, thumping a fist on his father's bedroom door. "Can you drive me to school today?"

Because otherwise he has to take the bus, and that means seeing Eddie.

Dad's door opens, and there's the man himself, bearded and squinting one eye at him, the other closed tight against the angry daylight of the morning. "Why?"

"I missed the bus," Terence says.

Dad looks back into the bedroom at his clock on the nightstand. "No, you didn't."

"I plan to."

Dad sighs. "Get dressed. Go to school. Leave me alone." With that, he closes the door.

Ten minutes later, Terence is slogging on his bike through a sleety morning with the wind in his face.

"Hey." It's Eddie, of course. She's caught him between classes and snuck up from behind.

Terence doesn't turn around. He just moves to the side of the hallway and leans on someone's locker.

"You didn't reply to a single text this weekend," Eddie says.

"Sorry."

"You don't have to be embarrassed," she says quietly at his ear. He can feel her breath on his neck.

"I'm not."

Eddie is quiet for a second.

"I have to get to class," Terence says.

"You're next class is lunch," Eddie says. "Sit with me."

Terence shakes his head. "I'm not going to lunch," he says, and quickly adds, "I'm going to the media center. I have a lot of homework to do."

"Liar."

Terence shrugs and steps away, weaving through the river of other students toward the library.

The problem with hiding during lunch in the media center is that there's no eating allowed in there, and even if there were, Terence doesn't have any food with him.

His stomach, though, is used to eating at 11:30, so at 11:32 it starts rumbling. To distract himself, he pulls on headphones and opens his email to check out that MP3 from Eddie.

It's solo piano. He knows the piece at once: "Für Elise," by Beethoven. Every piano student learns it at some point. He never studied piano with the top players at Hart, but he's pretty sure even he can muddle his way through it.

Still, he can tell this player is good. Then again, Melody was good too, and can probably play "Für Elise" with her eyes closed with one hand while playing Chopin with the other hand.

Then suddenly it changes. Something just clicks, and the player starts weaving in and out of "Für Elise," threading through the song with jazzy fills, improvised little licks. It starts to swing a little, nothing like old Ludwig Van ever imagined.

By the time the finale comes along, it has a bebop, funky feel like the great jazz pianist Thelonious Monk, barely recognizable as "Für Elise," but the themes are still there if you know what to listen for.

Terence pulls off the headphones and notices others in the media center staring at him. When he looks back, a girl stage-whispers, "You were tapping your foot."

The media specialist, Mr. W, appears next to his chair. "Loudly," he says.

"Oh," Terence says as his face goes hot, "sorry."

Mr. W shakes his head slowly and clicks his tongue before stepping away.

Terence clicks "reply" in his email from Eddie and writes, *Who is it?*

It only takes a moment for Eddie to reply, which means she's in the cafeteria just down the hall with her phone in her hands: *You have to meet him. Come to Paulie's tonight?*

Paulie's is the pizza place on Old Main Street. Everyone knows it, and Terence loves the pizza there. But he doesn't reply. He just closes his email and logs out of the computer.

"Dad?" Terence says when he arrives home from school. He's early. It's easy to be early getting home — even on your bike — if you sneak out before last bell.

After a quick search of the little rented house, and to Terence's complete surprise, Dad isn't home.

"I guess that means he at least got dressed today," Terence mutters to himself as he pulls out his phone. "Or he went out in his bathrobe."

Eddie has peppered Terence with texts most of the afternoon. Around now, she's probably climbing onto the bus for the ride home, maybe wondering if Terence will show up. The phone vibrates again in his hand as he looks at it.

Another from Eddie: *You're not on the bus.*

He types back: *I'm not?! Weird!*, and laughs.

Just be at Paulie's, smarty-pants, she texts back. *7 sharp!!*

Terence taps off the screen and tosses his phone onto the bed. He opens his laptop and pulls up the MP3 Eddie sent him earlier and plays it again. It really is good.

Maybe Dad will give him a ride to Paulie's.

CHAPTER TWELVE

Or maybe not.

At 6:45, it's dark and freezing cold as Terence pushes his pedals against icy winds and slushy sidewalks toward Old Main. Terence texted Dad, and he waited as long as he could for him to come home, but then he had no choice: if he wanted to meet this pianist, he'd have to bike.

By the time Paulie's big neon sign comes into view and he can smell the garlic-oil-brushed crust, his eyes are running against the cold and his nostrils are nearly sealed with frozen snot.

Terence pulls off his gloves to lock up his bike to the rack out front. When he's done, his fingers sting. He walks into Paulie's a little after seven, wiping his eyes and nose and blowing into his fists to warm his hands.

It seems like everyone in the little restaurant looks up at him in the doorway as he's unzipping his parka. Maybe it's just everyone at Eddie's table: Eddie, facing him with a forkful of lettuce halfway to her mouth, Luke, a woman who must be their mom, and a big guy with his back to the door.

Terence walks to their table. "Um," he says, wondering where he'll sit, "hi."

Eddie puts down her fork and grins as she stands. "You made it!" she says, and introduces him around the table. The big guy is Claude.

"Wait, *he's* the guy on the MP3?" Terence says, backing away a little. "Nope. No way."

"What MP3?" Claude says.

Terence squints at Eddie a second before turning his back on the table and heading for the door.

"Terry!" Eddie shouts. Her chair scrapes as she pushes it back to hurry after him.

Terence stops with his hand on the door handle.

"Just give him a chance," she says, a hand on his shoulder.

"Do you know two big gorillas knocked me down this morning?" Terence says without turning around.

"Who?"

"How should I know?" Terence says. "I don't know anyone at this dumb school besides you . . . and Melody Ulrich. I just know they were big dumb jerks."

"Like my brother," Eddie says.

Terence shrugs and looks through the door's window at the darkness outside. It's started to snow.

"Terry, I—"

"Terence," he says.

After a moment, Eddie goes on, "Terence, sorry. Just sit and have pizza. Claude's a nice guy. He's just . . . big."

"And your brother?"

"I mean, he can be a jerk," Eddie admits, "but he won't. Not to you. Not to my friend."

Terence shoots her a glance over his shoulder at the word "friend."

"Sorry," she corrects. "My bandmate."

Terence turns around and almost laughs.

"Come on," Eddie says. "Have pizza. And no sulking, OK? My mom can't stand sulking."

"There aren't enough chairs."

But when he glances at the table, the waiter — a high school kid with a nametag that says "James" — is placing a chair between Eddie and her mom's seat for Terence.

"Oh."

"Come on."

So he does.

The pizza is great, as always, and by eight o'clock he's eaten his fill, had three Cokes, and even laughed a couple of times at Luke's stupid jokes.

When they all bundle up and step out into the frigid night, Terence thanks Eddie's mom for dinner. He heads for his bike.

"Wait a minute, Terence," her mom says, jogging after him, holding her knitted scarf over her mouth and nose. "You *biked* here?"

"He bikes everywhere," Eddie says. "He's a maniac."

"Well, not on my watch," her mom says. "We'll drive you home."

"Mom," Eddie says. "We walked."

Her mom looks at Terence a moment. "We live close," she says. "Walk your bike with us, and we can put it in the back of the SUV and drive you home from there."

"Really, it's no problem," Terence says.

"No way," Eddie's mom says. "You're coming with us. I insist."

Eddie's family lives very close, and after a five-minute walk with his bike and motley companions, Terence lets Eddie lean the bike beside the front stoop and lead him inside.

Eddie kicks off her boots. "I'm glad you joined us for pizza, at least."

"Me too," Terence admits. "And Claude seems OK, I guess."

"You guess?"

Terence laughs. "We should ask him to play with us."

Eddie nods. "I already have," she admits. "Tomorrow afternoon before jazz band in Mr. Bonk's room. I got his permission."

"Were you planning to tell me?" Terence protests.

Eddie giggles. "I just did. Is your bass still in Bonk's office."

Terence nods.

"OK then," she says as Mom comes in. "See you tomorrow!" With that, she scurries up a narrow staircase.

"OK, Terence," Mom says as she pokes around in the depths of her huge purse. "Let's see if we can get you home."

"Thanks," he says.

"I cannot . . . find . . . my car keys," she says, looking up and smiling at him just like Eddie does. "Give me one minute, OK?" She hurries down the hall into the kitchen.

Terence sits on the bottom of the steps, and from above he hears a slightly out-of-tune guitar being strummed.

It's Eddie, obviously, practicing in her room probably.

She's not very good. The chord changes are uninspired and the strumming is not rhythmic. It sounds like her fingers are pretty weak too, unable to hold the strings tight against the fret board. But Terence knows that will get better with practice.

Then, though, she begins to sing. Terence doesn't recognize the song. It must be one of hers. The melody is beautiful. The lyrics — when he can make them out — are better than he would have thought.

He's on his feet, looking up the stairs, straining to hear better, when Eddie's mom comes back down the hall, jangling her keys.

"Ready, Terence?" she says, snapping his musical reverie.

"Oh, yes," he says. "Thanks again."

A few minutes later, Terence is strapped into the front seat of the Carson family's SUV, the heated seat warming him and a hot breeze blowing in his face from the gleaming dash.

His bike — the tires caked in slush — bangs around in the back.

"So, Terence," Ms. Carson says, "Meredith tells me you just started at Franklin?"

"That's right."

"You were at Hart Arts?" Ms. Carson asks. "Impressive."

"I guess," Terence says, but he's wishing she'd stop. Small talk like this can often lead to big talk, and big talk he'd much rather avoid.

"How many instruments do you play?" she asks as the SUV rolls slowly along Route 116. The roads are bad, and she can't even go the speed limit. Still, his house isn't far. This might be OK.

"Five, altogether," Terence says. "Some better than others."

"That is amazing," Ms. Carson says. "I'm so proud of my kids for staying interested in music. Though I don't know if Luke will stick with his sax much longer."

No great loss there, Terence thinks.

"So why did you leave Hart?" Ms. Carson says as she turns onto 18th Avenue.

Maybe he can get out here and bike the rest.

"Oh, um," Terence says, "we just couldn't afford the tuition anymore. It's pretty expensive."

"Yeah, I've heard that," Ms. Carson says, forcing a smile and glancing at Terence as the corner closest to Terence's rental house comes into view.

She turns left, and Terence leans forward in his seat. "It's the little blue one," he says, pointing through the windshield. "After the brick one on the right."

Ms. Carson pulls up to the curb and switches off the engine. "I'll help you with your bike."

"Oh, I'm fine," Terence says, climbing out.

"Don't be ridiculous," Ms. Carson says as she meets Terence at the back of the SUV and pops open the tailgate. Together they lift the filthy bike from the car and set it on the sidewalk. "There you go."

"Thanks again, Ms. Carson," Terence says, "and thanks for dinner."

"My pleasure," Ms. Carson says as Terence pushes his bike toward the house. "And Terence? If you ever need anything, you let us know, OK?"

"O-OK," Terence stammers.

"Eddie told me about your mother," Ms. Carson adds quickly, practically shouting across the yard to him. "I'm very sorry."

Terence stops and looks at the gray muck clinging to his bike tires. He never knows what to say when grown-ups apologize for his mom being dead, like it's their fault, or like they stepped on his toe.

So he doesn't say anything. He just waits a moment, and then she says, "Well, goodbye, Terence. Very nice to meet you."

"Bye," Terence manages to push out, and he watches as she climbs back into the SUV and drives slowly away.

CHAPTER THIRTEEN

"You know, Terence," Mr. Bonk says, his arms folded high across his chest, his chin up and his mustache shaking ferociously, "if it's a band you're looking for, we've got one here at Franklin Middle. You remember, don't you?"

"I know," Terence says, wishing Eddie and Claude would show up so he could edge his way out of this awkward conversation. "I just don't think I'll have the time, and—"

"Hey, Mr. Bonk!" Eddie bellows as she shoves through the double doors to the band room. Claude trails a few steps behind her, his mouth half open, his hair a mop over his bulging forehead.

Terence can hardly believe this is the same boy who played that amazing rendition of "Für Elise."

"Ms. Carson," Mr. Bonk says as his shoulders sag. "You have fifteen minutes."

"Thanks, Mr. B!" Eddie says as the walrusy teacher steps into his office and closes the door.

"He does *not* like me," Terence says.

"Really?" Eddie says, grinning. "'Cause I'm pretty sure I just chased him out of the room by saying hi."

"He's not a big fan of mine, either," Claude says as he settles onto the piano bench at the front of the room. As if to punctuate his speech, he runs rapid-fire through a couple of jazzy scales. "He learned a few weeks ago that I play but never joined band."

"Why didn't you?" Terence says as he plugs in his bass.

Claude shrugs as he plays the opening to "Straight, No Chaser." "I have football practice every afternoon in the fall," he says, staring straight ahead, as if he's not just banging out a Thelonious Monk classic like it's nothing, "and hockey practice all winter."

Terence picks up the bass part, and they jam on the old jazz standard for a minute. But while the song got some lyrics in the 1980s — thirty years after Monk wrote the instrumental version — most singers don't know them.

"OK, let's bring Eddie in," Terence says over the music, and Claude stops, clinks a few keys idly, and then launches into a jaunty, up-tempo chord change. Terence picks up the strolling bass line.

Eddie looks confused.

"'All of Me!'" Terence calls to her over the music, and as it dawns on her she nods, her eyes wide, and then she sings, her voice somewhere between Billie Holliday and Sarah Vaughn: raspy and young, but with Sarah Vaughn's power and bombast.

Eddie snaps her fingers as she paces between Terence and Claude's piano. Before long, Mr. Bonk's door opens and he stands in the doorway, shaking his head to the rhythm, a sorrowful frown on his face, forlorn that none of this trio are in his jazz band.

"All right, that was great," Terence says when the song ends.

Mr. Bonk waves dismissively at the new bandmates and retreats into his office again.

"Yeah, that was fun," Claude says. "You guys ever do anything a little . . ."

"More rock?" Terence finishes for him, and Claude nods. "Like what?"

Claude chews his cheek, staring past Terence. He really does look like a big dumb kid, but Terence is starting to see how deceiving appearances can be.

A flash of recognition crosses Claude's face, and he quietly sounds out a couple of chords before banging them out like a honky-tonk maniac.

"We need a guitar for that!" Terence says over the din.

"Fake it!" Claude shouts back, smiling a little.

And Terence does his best, which might not be enough, since Claude is playing the opening chords of Led Zeppelin's "South Bound Saurez." That means Terence has to somehow play John Paul Jones's thumping bass line at the same time as Jimmy Page's sliding and syncopated riff.

That means he has to knock the E string on every sixteenth note, while his pinky works on the higher strings to do a passable imitation of Page's guitar. It's not ideal.

To his surprise, though, just as he hits the first chord change, Eddie steps between him and Claude and belts out an amazing Robert Plant impression. It sounds pretty good.

In fact, it sounds *great*.

They're halfway through — Terence and Claude almost laughing at Eddie's vocal antics — when Mr. Bonk appears again, this time far less impressed and waving his arms over his head.

Eddie stops singing. Terence stops playing. Claude

keeps on, since his back is to Bonk's door. He looks at Terence, confused, as he reaches the guitar solo and starts in on a wild improvisation of his own.

"Claude Viateur!" Mr. Bonk shouts.

Claude stops and turns around on the bench. "Oh, sorry. Is our time up?"

Mr. Bonk's face is red enough to pop, Terence thinks.

"Um, yes," Terence says, dropping to one knee and unplugging his bass. "Packing up now, Mr. Bonk."

Mr. Bonk stares the three bandmates down for a moment before heading back into his office, mumbling under his breath something about "rock and roll *garbage*" as he closes the door.

"So you're in?" Terence says, walking between Eddie and Claude up the ramp toward the exit. His bass hangs from one shoulder in its gig bag, Mr. Bonk having made him take it with him this time.

Terence and Eddie will have to catch the late bus in an hour. Claude has to hurry to the gym to change for hockey practice.

"Yeah," Claude says. "It could be fun, and I don't get any time to play what I like. My folks have me practicing sonatas all the time with Ms. Kilpatrick."

"*Arlene* Kilpatrick?" Terence says.

"You know her?" Claude asks, surprised.

"Sure, she teaches at Hart," Terence says, remembering Kilpatrick's wicked Advanced Theory course from that fall.

"She's tough," the boys say at the same time.

Terence laughs.

Eddie gives him a shove with her shoulder. "Don't forget the band rule," she says.

"What?" Terence says.

"You know," Eddie says. "The *one rule.*"

Terence thinks a minute and remembers. "Right," he says firmly. "Not looking for friends."

Claude glances at Eddie. "OK then," he says.

At the top of the ramp, he heads toward the gym. "See you guys," he says.

"Have fun!" Eddie calls after.

Friends or not, Terence is pleased. His band is starting to come together, and with players more talented than he ever imagined he'd find at a public school.

So when he bumps into another kid in the glare of sunshine through the glass front doors, he's smiling. "Oh, excuse me," he says as he looks up —

— right into the faces of his two bullies from the other morning.

"Oh," he says, backing away. "Look, guys, I—"

But they're not interested in chatting. With two

hands, one of them shoves him backward, so he stumbles at the top of the ramp and falls onto his butt. His bass lands next to him with a thud. Terence hopes it's not damaged.

"Hey!" Eddie says, running to help him. But the other bully grabs her by the wrist and moves her aside.

"Just mind your own business, *Edward*," he says as his partner in crime moves in on Terence, kicking his foot.

"You gonna get up?" the bully asks.

Terence shakes his head.

"That's what I thought," he says. "Didn't we tell you we don't want to see you around here anymore?"

"Yeah," says the one who has Eddie by the wrist. "Go back to Harts and Farts."

"Jerks!" Eddie says, trying to pull her wrist away. The bullies just laugh at her.

"Now, how are we gonna punish this weirdo for not following our orders?" says the bully standing over Terence.

As he leans down, his fists primed, Terence covers his face and closes his eyes.

"You're not," comes a deep and terrifying voice.

Terence opens his eyes, and there's Claude standing between the two bullies with one giant, piano-playing hand on each of their throats. The bullies' eyes are wide in terror, though it doesn't look like he's squeezing hard.

He must have a reputation, then.

"Understand?" Claude says.

The bullies nod and gasp "yes," and when he releases them, they bolt down the hall and out of sight.

"You OK?" he says, helping Terence up.

"I think so," Terence says. "Um, thanks."

"Sure," Claude says, clapping his hands together as if dusting them off. "That's what friends are for, right?"

Claude grins and corrects himself, "I mean bandmates."

Eddie laughs and grabs Terence's arm. "Come on," she says. "You're making Claude late for hockey practice."

Claude gives Terence a light punch on the shoulder before hurrying away again.

"So?" Eddie says.

"So?" Terence says.

"Maybe we're friends a *tiny* bit?" Eddie says, her smile and eyes twinkling.

Terence adjusts the strap of his gig bag on his shoulder. "A tiny bit," he admits, and he lets himself smile as the two of them step outside into the chilly and sunny winter afternoon to wait for the late bus.

PART

THREE

CHAPTER FOURTEEN

It's Sunday night, and Terence couldn't be happier with the band so far.

Claude's piano playing is on fire tonight.

Eddie's vocals are rich and lovely as a devil's food cake covered in honey.

Terence rethinks his metaphor, but the band is sounding great even in the crummy acoustics of Claude's basement practice room, which is nowhere near as impressive or state-of-the-art as that of Melody Ulrich.

Still, he's a lot more pleasant to be around than Melody, once again reminding Terence that his ability to judge people based on appearance is woefully inadequate. Plus there was that whole probably-saving-Terence's-life thing.

Bullying was never a problem back at Hart. But at a public middle school with a huge student population, it's bound to come up. And for Terence Kato, it has.

But that was last week. Ever since Claude stepped in just in the nick of time, the two colossal brutes haven't even looked sideways at Terence.

Claude ends their rendition of "Firework" with a piano flourish. It's not Terence's favorite song, but it was on his band's playlist at Hart. Polly Winger always rocked it, and it was always a big crowd pleaser.

Eddie rocks it too.

"Great job, guys," Terence says.

"Thanks, boss," Eddie says with a wink at Claude. Claude snickers and covers the laughter with a fast arpeggio.

"Laugh if you want," Terence says as he unplugs his bass. "But someone needs to take the wheel."

"Says who?" Eddie says, sneering at him.

"Says me," Terence says. He lays his bass carefully in its case. "And I'm the only one of us who's been in a band before, right?"

Eddie shrugs. "I guess."

"So get us a gig," Claude says, getting back to his arpeggios.

"We're not ready for gigs," Terence says, almost laughing. "For one thing, we still need a guitar player and dru—"

"What?" Claude says, finishing a scale with a dramatic A-minor chord. "We don't need a guitar player. I can handle everything right here on the ivories."

Terence shakes his head as he winds his cord and lays it on top of his bass case. "The set list has too much old soul, R&B, and rock to have no guitar. Beside, I love a guitar in a jazz combo too. Joe Pass? Wes Montgomery?"

Claude stares at him blankly. He glances at Eddie.

She cocks her head. "I have *Take Love Easy* on vinyl." That's the first duet album with Joe Pass and Ella Fitzgerald, possibly the best vocalist of all time, in jazz or otherwise.

Terence flashes an impressed face and gets to his feet, his gig bag over his shoulder. "The point is, we need a guitar player."

"Well," Claude says, leaning back and cracking his knuckles, "lots of people play guitar."

"I play guitar," Eddie says.

"But most aren't very good," Claude says, looking at Eddie with a crooked grin.

"Point taken," Eddie admits.

"Well," Terence says, "I'll ask around again. Though that didn't end very well when I tried to find a pianist."

"So leave it to us," Claude says as he rises from the piano bench to see his bandmates out.

"Yeah," Eddie says. "We know all these kids already. And we wouldn't want you to put yourself in danger of making a *friend*."

Claude laughs, and Terence feels his face go hot. *Rule number one,* he thinks.

It's just easier without friends — especially when you consider why he left Hart Arts to begin with: dead mother, no money, and a dad who has completely checked out.

"That's fine with me," Terence says, and though his bass is heavy, he feels a weight lift from his shoulder. "The fewer people I have to talk to, the better."

"I heard you're looking for a guitar player," says a whispery voice at Terence's ear in advisory first thing Monday morning.

"Um," Terence says, keeping his eyes on the open book on his desk. It's a kind of how-to book on the bassists who played with funk, R&B, and soul great James Brown over the years, some of the best players in music history. "Where'd you hear that?"

He glances quickly to his right. It's a girl he knows — kind of. After all, he's been sitting next to her in advisory for two weeks now. *Sophia? Ophelia, maybe?*

"I overheard your friend Eddie asking a couple of seventh graders if they knew any guitarists," the girl whispers. "And she said she wants a girl."

Terence looks up. "A girl?" he says. "Why?"

"So she's not outnumbered?" the girl replies, shrugging. "I assume."

"Huh." Terence looks back at his book.

After a moment of silence, the girl asks, "So are you? Looking?"

Terence nods.

The girl scoots her chair a little closer. "You like James Brown?"

"Doesn't everyone?"

"I don't think most kids at this school know who James Brown is, Terry," the girl says.

So she knows his name. Sort of.

"I actually prefer Terence," he says, closing his book. "You'd have to audition."

She nods eagerly and smiles. "Of course."

"Can you stay after school a few minutes?"

She shakes her head. "I have lessons this afternoon."

She takes guitar lessons, Terence thinks. *I guess at least she's serious.* "Tomorrow?"

She shakes her head again. "After my lessons today," she says. "Like five?"

Terence thinks about the bike ride in the cold,

assuming his dad is no help again. He sighs. "Sure, I can do that. Where do you live?"

The girl tears the corner off a sheet of paper from her notebook and scribbles down her address.

Terence takes the paper and reads her name at the top. "Novia."

"That's me," she says. A moment later the bell rings to end advisory. "See you at five."

CHAPTER FIFTEEN

"I'm home!" Terence says as he walks into the rental house and drops his book bag next to the door.

He almost expects silence in response. He's gotten so used to Dad not being around, or being asleep or half asleep in front of the TV when he is around.

So when Dad walks out of the little kitchen at the back of the house dressed in khakis and a collared shirt, Terence is stunned.

"How was your day?" Dad says as if it's the most normal thing in the world to say.

Which it is, of course — but not for Dad lately.

"Fine," Terence says, leaning on the back of the couch. It's the couch from their old house: the color of milk chocolate, soft and leather, so no matter how many times and how often Terence has tried, he can't find the scent of Mom's perfume anymore. The smell of the leather is too strong. "Can you drive me to a friend's in an hour or so?"

Dad grins and puts an arm around Terence's shoulders. "I'm so pleased you're making friends at your new school," he says.

Terence shrugs and pulls away. "So can you?"

"Sure," Dad says. He drops into his chair by the front window. It's also from the old house, as luxurious as the couch. Dad reclines and pulls out his phone.

"Um, Dad?" Terence says as he sits on the edge of the couch.

His father looks up from his phone and smiles. Terence hasn't seen that smile in months. Maybe that's why it looks so funny.

"What's going on with you?" Terence asks.

Dad's smile freezes, not that it was moving and animated before. It just suddenly seems to be made of ice or something. Just as quickly, it shatters, and there's Dad's familiar flat frown. "I'm sorry," is all he says as he sits forward in his chair.

Terence leans back, and his head sinks into the leather couch cushions. The couch seems to exhale as the pillows give way to his weight.

"I've been depressed," Dad says. "Obviously. I'm — I'm having a hard time. And I haven't been much of a parent."

Terence sits up quickly. "I don't mean that," he says, and he wants to go on, but Dad cuts him off.

"It's fine. You're right." Dad puts his face in his hands, and soon he's silently sobbing, his shoulders bucking and the occasional croak escaping between his hands.

It's been a while since Dad cried in front of him — a few months at least. Terence is beside him and sitting on the arm of the recliner in moments, one arm around his dad. The first few times this happened after Mom died, it took him completely by surprise, and Terence sobbed right along with him.

Now, though, Terence has numbed to the outbursts, almost as if his job is to make sure Dad gets it out of his system quickly and remembers Terence is there with him.

It works, and after less than a minute, Dad stops croaking and pulls his face out of his hands. He takes a deep breath, staring into his still-open palms. "Sorry."

"It's OK," Terence says quietly.

Dad falls back in the recliner — his face flat, his eyes rimmed in red — and Terence hurries to his room. Hopefully when it's time to go to Novia's house, Dad will be back to wearing that frozen smile; riding with Dad — when he's sobbing or exhausted from sobbing — always reminds Terence of Mom's funeral back in July.

It was a hot day, and Terence sat sweating in a big black car in his too-big black suit with a black tie squeezing his neck too tight beside his father.

They held hands over the chasm of seat between them, and Dad held his handkerchief in his other hand. His eyes were already red and heavy and tired from crying when he said, "What are we gonna do, Ter-bear?"

Terence's little-kid pet name. Mom and Dad stopped using it years before.

But Terence didn't answer. He looked out the car window at the city on that Sunday — a regular day for everyone else.

It's five after five when Terence climbs out of the front seat of Dad's car. "You sure you don't mind waiting?" he says, leaning in the open door.

"Nah," Dad says. He holds up his phone. "I've got shows to catch up on."

"I won't be more than ten minutes," Terence says.

"I'll leave it running," Dad says, patting the dashboard near the heater knobs.

"You can probably come inside," Terence says. "If you want."

Dad seems to think about it for a moment, but he shakes his head. "Not much in the mood to meet parents and make small talk."

Terence understands that, and he closes the door and hurries down the path and onto the porch. The inner door opens right away, but it's not Novia. It's a middle-aged woman with short brown hair and glasses with cat's-eye frames.

"Oh, excuse me," she says.

"Is Novia home?" Terence asks, stopping in front of her.

"Um, yes," she says, stepping around Terence. "We just finished her lesson. Excuse me." With that, she leaves the porch, climbs into the little hatchback parked at the curb in front of Dad, and drives away.

Novia appears in the doorway a moment later. "Oh, there you are," she says. "Come on in."

"I thought that was your mom," Terence says.

Novia laughs. "That's Priscilla, my music teacher."

Terence is surprised to hear that woman is a guitar player, but he doesn't say so. He just follows Novia inside. "Mom, my friend's here to hear me play guitar!"

Her mom calls back from somewhere deep inside the house, "OK! Keep the door open! Good luck!"

Novia looks at Terence and rolls her eyes. "Come on," she says, heading up the narrow stairs.

Terence follows her up and into her bedroom. It's narrow as well, with only a long desk on one side and a twin bed on the other. A small window between lets in some light until Novia flicks on the lamp, and the window is more like a little mirror at the end of the room.

Terence catches his own reflection in the window as he sits in the chair at the desk, and Novia drops to one knee to open her guitar case.

"So," Terence says, watching her pull out the acoustic guitar and check the tuning, "what do you like to play?"

"My mom taught me a bunch of folky nineties songs," Novia says as she sits on the edge of the bed and plays a big open G chord. She adds a seventh and plays it again. She adds a ninth and plays it again.

"Do you know any jazz?" Terence asks. So far, Novia doesn't seem promising to join the band. "Can you improvise at all?"

She twists up her mouth. "Not really," she admits. "I've only been playing for six months."

Six months? Terence thinks. *Why is she wasting my time?*

"I'm naturally pretty musical, though," she says as she strums the chord changes to what might be an Indigo Girls song. "I'm sure I'll pick it up quickly."

"Mmhm," Terence says.

Novia shifts on the edge of the bed, fixes her hair, and then starts a song in earnest: "Stubborn Love" by the Lumineers. Terence isn't a big fan. Novia's voice is pleasant enough, but the guitar part is simple and folky, not at all the sort of music Terence wants for his band.

She plays through the first chorus and then stops. "What do you think?" she says, looking at Terence.

"Very good," he says. "You have a nice voice. But I don't know if your guitar playing is right for what we're doing."

"Oh," Novia says, obviously disappointed.

Terence stands. "Yeah," he says, pushing his hand through his hair and wondering how soon he can leave. "I mean, you obviously like folk music and stuff, but we're really — that is, we're looking for a real *virtuoso*, you know?"

Novia shrugs as she lays her guitar in its case.

"But stick with the lessons for sure," Terence says, moving toward the door. "You're doing great for only having played six months."

Novia closes the case as Terence starts to back down the stairs. "I don't take guitar lessons," she says.

"Oh, but . . . ," Terence starts. "I thought—"

Novia stops in the doorway and looks down the stairs at Terence. "You can let yourself out," she says and closes the door to her bedroom.

"How'd it go?" Dad asks when Terence gets into the front seat of the warm car.

"Fine," Terence says. "She's not good enough for the band though."

"Oh, too bad," Dad says, putting the car in drive. "I hope you let her down easy."

"I tried to," Terence says.

Dad pulls away from the curb, and Terence texts Eddie: *Any luck finding a guitarist?*

A moment later her reply comes: *Claude found someone to play this weekend.*

Then, a few seconds later she texts again: *He's REALLY good.*

CHAPTER SIXTEEN

He is really good.

It's Saturday morning. The band is in Claude's basement again, and this time they have their fourth: Desmond, a long-haired, pale boy in a black hoodie with a sleek black guitar slung around his neck and shoulders.

His changes are quick and tight. He plays along with Terence's jazzy bass line with no problem, following the tough changes. He's as good at guitar as Claude is at piano and Terence is at bass. Eddie sits to the side, nodding along with the music and sometimes smiling.

So far, so good.

"Let's trade fours awhile," Terence says over the music.

Claude leaps into a wild, modal solo, banging away at the keys like only a jazz pianist can. When he's done, Terence picks it up and runs the neck, following Claude's modal lead but keeping it smooth instead of the choppy Thelonious Monk style Claude prefers on the keys.

He looks over at Desmond and nods as he reaches the end of his fourth measure, and Desmond flicks the knob on his guitar, sending the volume into the stratosphere, and then blasts off like a rocket into a mind-numbing and ear-piercing heavy-metal guitar solo.

Terence looks over at Claude on the piano as Desmond's fingers tap nearly every fret on his board, sounding more like Yngwie Malmsteen than Joe Pass. Claude shrugs back at him. Eddie's eyes go wide, and she leans back as if the blast of the guitar solo is a gust of wind.

As he plays his four-bar solo, he bangs his head up and down, sending his hair in a circular whip. His fingers are lightning across the fretboard. He's skilled, fast, talented — but it's not right for the song at all.

When he's done, Terence puts up a hand and closes his fist to the end the jam. A moment later, they hear Claude's mother call down the basement steps. "Everything OK down there?"

"Yeah, Mom!" Claude shouts back. "Why?"

"It sounded like World War Three broke out!" she shouts back.

Desmond laughs. "That was nothing!"

"Um, right," Claude says. He calls up to his mom, "Sorry! We're just finishing up."

"That's a relief," his mom replies. The basement door closes.

Terence unplugs his bass. "Thanks for playing with us, Desmond," he says. "That solo was something."

"Yeah!" Eddie says, jumping up from her seat. "That rocked."

"Thanks, guys," Desmond says as he packs up his guitar.

Claude rises from the piano bench and stands over Desmond, who kneels in the center of the room, zipping up his case. "We'll let you know," Claude says, his voice deep and menacing.

Desmond stands as he backs away. "OK," he says, his voice trembling a bit. "Thanks."

With that, he hurries up the steps. They hear the muffled sounds of Claude's mom saying goodbye and the front door closing.

"You didn't have to scare him like that," Eddie says.

Claude shrugs. "Rejection is tough," he says. "Might as well make myself as scary as possible so he doesn't remember the part about having his feelings hurt."

"That," Terence says, "actually makes a little sense. It's twisted and bizarre, but it makes sense."

Claude laughs as he sits at the piano again. "Let's get that metal garbage out of our system."

"It wasn't *that* bad," Eddie says quietly.

"It was," Claude insists. He plays a quick chromatic run up the piano keyboard, and in moments Terence joins in. Before long, they're jamming on Terence's chord changes. Eddie even joins in with improvised lyrics and scatting.

It's fun. And they sound *good*.

Eddie is grinning and having a blast. Claude looks over at Terence, his eyebrows high and his smile wide. Soon Claude's mom comes down the stairs, and they stop midjam.

"Sorry, Mom," Claude says. "We'll stop now."

"What?" she says, smiling. "I came down to watch and listen. You three sound fantastic!"

"We do, don't we?" Terence says.

"See?" Claude says. "We don't need a guitarist. We're a trio. It works."

"Especially that guitarist," Claude's mom says as she goes back up the stairs. "He scared me."

Terence thinks a moment. They do sound good as a trio. Sure, a few of the songs in the set list need a guitar, but maybe the set list could stand some editing anyway.

"OK," Terence says, "then it's settled. We're a trio."

Eddie grins. Claude plays a celebratory arpeggio. "Let's celebrate," he says.

"Paulie's!" Eddie says. She grabs her bag from the old couch behind the piano.

"My treat!" Claude's mom calls down the steps.

"Mom!" Claude shouts. "You were eavesdropping!"

"What?" she replies, sticking her head through the doorway at the top of the steps. "I'm excited!

CHAPTER SEVENTEEN

The three bandmates and Claude's mom slide into their favorite booth at Paulie's. "Order anything you like," says Claude's mom as she rises again. "I have to visit the little girl's room." She winks and hurries away.

"I need pineapple," Eddie says.

"On pizza?" Claude says, looking up from his menu. "That's literally a sin."

"They do it in Hawaii," Eddie says.

"Actually, I think they put SPAM on pizza in Hawaii," Terence says.

"What?" Eddie says, practically sneering at him. "That's ridiculous."

A moment later, their server steps up to the table.

It's James, the sixteen-year-old server they had last time they were in, when Terence first met Claude.

"Oh, it's you three again," he says. "Where's your Neanderthal big brother?" he adds, sneering at Eddie.

"Oh, hi, James," Eddie says, her voice making it very clear that she's choosing the high road this time. "Having a nice Saturday?"

"Yeah, it's great," he says sarcastically. "I love taking orders from children and carrying hot pizza trays all day. What do you want?"

"We haven't decided yet," Eddie says, flashing a big and phony grin. "Why don't you come back in two minutes to check again?"

James grins back and then rolls his eyes as he puts his pencil behind his ear and walks off.

"He's a pleasure," Terence says.

"Always," Eddie says, shaking her head.

As Claude's mom returns to the booth and slides in next to her son, the front door swings open, letting in the winter sunshine along with a family of five — including Novia, the girl Terence met earlier that week.

She immediately spots Terence, makes a quick surprised and disgusted face, and hurries along with her family toward their table in the back.

"Ugh," Terence says, letting his head drop onto the red plaid tablecloth with a thud.

"Oh my," Claude's mom says.

"You know Novia?" Eddie says, leaning close to Terence's face on the table.

Terence lifts his head and nods. "She's the guitarist I auditioned the other night," he says. "I told her she wasn't right for the band . . . but I think she could tell I really meant she wasn't good enough."

"Novia Pagano plays guitar too?" Claude says, squinting at Terence in confusion.

James steps up to the table and smiles at Claude's mom. "Are you folks ready to order?" he asks, all smiles.

While Claude's mom places the order, Terence leans across the table a little and says quietly to Claude. "What do you mean, 'too'?"

Claude's mom finishes the order — a large pizza, half plain, half pineapple and ham, and a pitcher of pop — and then interrupts before Claude can reply. "Novia Pagano plays harp for the Catholic church."

"Harp?" Terence says.

"Sure, everyone knows that," Eddie says. "She's been taking lessons forever."

"Oh," Terence says. "That lady was her harp teacher, not guitar teacher."

Eddie nods. "She's had a special solo in the holiday concert at the middle school for the last three years too. Didn't you see it in December?"

"Um, wasn't here yet," Terence says, "remember?"

"Oh, right," Eddie says. She shoves him gently. "I keep forgetting you're the new kid."

Terence rolls his eyes. "So she's really good?"

Claude nods. "Amazing."

His mom nods too.

Terence looks across the restaurant. He can see the back of her head from where he's sitting — her long black hair hanging over her shoulders and halfway down her back. When she turns her head and looks back at him, he quickly looks away.

"You know," Claude says, "it might sound pretty cool to have a harp in the group."

Terence has been thinking the exact same thing.

"Totally," Eddie says. She waves over at Novia.

"Don't!" Terence says, grabbing her hand to stop her. "Even if she wanted to play harp with our band, she hates me now. And who could blame her?"

"Not me," Eddie says.

"Me either," Claude agrees.

"Anyway, so what?" Eddie says. "Let her hate you. We're not friends, right?"

"Right," Terence says.

"Cool," Eddie says as James steps up to the table with the pitcher of pop and four cups. "I'll have to brush up on my Joanna Newsom lyrics."

"Just don't kill your dinner with karate while you're here," he says. "I'm not cleaning up after you."

"Joanna Newsom jokes," Terence says as Claude's mom pours drinks. "Kind of impressive."

"Yeah, it's my daydream to impress a bunch of kids with my encyclopedic musical knowledge," James says as he walks off.

"That guy," Eddie says staring daggers into his back. "Anyway, better go and ask Novia if she wants to play harp for us."

"What, me?" Terence says. "No way."

"Why not?" Eddie says.

"You know her better," Terence says. He looks at Claude. "You probably do too."

Claude takes a long drink of soda and then wipes his mouth with the back of his hand. "She goes to my church."

"Claude, use a napkin," his mom says, shoving one into his hand.

"Sorry, Mom."

Terence watches the exchange between mother and son, and he wants to smile and laugh and cry all at the same time. He shakes his head. "I can't do it. She hates me."

"Maybe if you apologize and invite her to join us, she won't hate you anymore," Eddie suggests.

"Oh, right," Terence says. "'Oh, hi, Novia. You remember me? Sorry I said you suck at guitar. Wanna play harp for us?' That'll go well."

"Fine," Eddie says, sliding out of the booth. "I'll do it. Baby."

Terence shrugs and watches Eddie weave between tables to the Paganos' booth. She talks to Novia for a moment. Of course Terence can't make out a word of it and he can't read lips.

But after a few words, both of them look back at Terence, and his face goes hot as he looks away.

When Eddie comes back, she slides in next to Terence — knocking into him a little too hard and obviously on purpose. "She'll do it," she says.

"She will?" Terence says, genuinely surprised.

"Hates you, though," Eddie says. "You were right about that."

She's not as mean to Terence as he fears though when she joins them in Claude's basement the next morning.

Not that he cares one way or the other, of course. He's not looking for friends. But he is looking for a great band.

And that he's got.

Novia's harp playing is lovely. At times he almost

feels redundant himself, since her fingers move over the strings of her harp, striking bass notes as often as treble.

They can work on that, and it'll be worth it. Her ear for modes and scales and improvising are flawless.

"So," Novia says after the song ends. She lowers her harp and looks squarely at Terence, "How'd I do?"

"Great," Terence says, forcing himself to look back at her. "That was fantastic."

"Thank you," Novia says, crossing her arms and leaning back a bit on her stool. "Now do you guys have a drummer, or . . . ?"

Terence, Eddie, and Claude exchange quick glances.

"Um, no," Terence says. "Why, do you think we need one?"

Novia shrugs and makes a bored *none of my business* face.

"My old band had a drummer," Terence says. "I'm not *against* it or anything." He looks at Eddie.

"I'm not against it either," she says. "But I don't know anyone."

"Yeah, you do," Claude says. "Henry Park is in jazz band with your brother."

"Oh, but he—" Eddie starts. She stops herself.

"He what?" Terence says.

"He's terrible," Claude says as his fingers move mindlessly and quietly over the keyboard.

"Like, he's a bad person?" Terence asks.

"Oh, no!" Eddie says quickly. "He's really nice."

"*Really* nice," Novia says.

"He's fine." Claude shrugs. "But he can't play."

"But he's in Bonk's jazz band?" Terence says.

The others nod.

"I don't understand," Terence admits.

"And finally the Hart Arts boy gets a glimpse of the seedy and untalented underbelly of public middle school music programs," Eddie says.

"So anyone who wants to join can just join?" Terence asks.

The others nod again.

"Huh," Terence says. "That's kinda nice, actually. It's not like they're playing halls or going on tour."

"Maybe we should try the high school," Claude says.

"What?" Eddie says. "No way."

Novia shakes her head. "No way. My brother is in high school. A senior. And no way. I don't want some greasy, smelly eighteen-year-old with a beard, and who probably smokes, hanging around."

Eddie points at Novia. "Mmhm. No way."

"Come on," Claude says, turning on his bench to argue with the girls. "We have no other option."

"What if we put an age limit," Terence says, "like sixteen?"

Eddie and Novia look at each other and seem to speak silently. Then they both nod. "Fine."

"If I make some flyers, can you ask your brother to hang them around the high school?" Terence says.

Novia bites her lip. "I guess," she says. "But that doesn't mean he'll do it."

"Good enough," Terence says. "I'll think of some other places to put them too."

Local band looking for drummer/percussion for jazz/rock/soul/R&B

Must be very good and 16 or younger. Must have your own kit.

Text Terence 952-555-0514

CHAPTER EIGHTEEN

First thing Monday morning, Terence grabs his phone to check for texts. Nothing — aside from one from Eddie: *Any texts yet???*

"Morning," Dad says when Terence drags himself into the kitchen. He's dressed in tan pants and a clean green sweater, and sitting at the table flipping through one of those thick magazines that just shows up at the house and no one ever ordered. A full cup of coffee sits steaming in the middle of the table. "Sleep OK?"

"Um, yeah. Fine," Terence says. "What are you doing up so early?"

"Can't a guy make breakfast for his son before school?" He puts the magazine down on the table.

"Theoretically, I guess," Terence says.

"What'll you have?"

"I'm not that hungry," Terence says.

'Oh, come on," Dad says, smiling as he gets up and goes to the fridge. "It's the most important meal of the day."

"A bagel, I guess," Terence says. "Half a bagel. With cream cheese."

"There we go," Dad says, opening the freezer and pulling out the plastic bag of bagels. "Coming right up."

They're both quiet for a minute while Dad pulls apart a frozen bagel, puts half in the toaster, and pushes it down.

"Dad," Terence says.

"Hm?" He gets the cream cheese tub and a knife.

"What's going on with you?" Terence asks.

"What do you mean?" Dad says without looking at him.

"For months you've been . . ."

"Depressed?"

"Yeah," Terence says. "I mean, I get that. But the last couple of days, you've been getting dressed, going out. I don't even know where you go some afternoons."

"Wait a second," Dad says, smirking. "Who's the dad here? You have to know where I am all the time?"

"That's not what I mean."

"I know," Dad says. The bagel pops up, and he quickly smears some cream cheese across its face. Then drops the plate in front of Terence's spot at the table and sits across from him.

Dad takes a deep breath and sighs. "I've been seeing a psychiatrist."

Terence stares down at the bagel. "Like, a therapist?"

Dad nods. "That's the general idea," he says. "I know I've been a mess since Mom passed, and it's not fair to you. It's not even fair to *me*."

Terence shrugs. He doesn't want Dad to think *his* sadness is hurting Terence somehow — though it is.

"So I decided to do something about it," Dad goes on. He runs a finger around the rim of his untouched coffee cup. "I've been to see Dr. Hyacinth four times so far. I think she's really helping."

"Good," Terence says, because what else can he say? It makes no sense that Dad acting a little happier and more normal has Terence feeling somehow even sadder than before.

Dad pushes his chair back and stands up. "Eat up," he says. "I'll give you a lift to school if you want. Got some errands to do this morning."

"OK." Terence takes a bite of his bagel, but when Dad's out of the room, he dumps it in the trash and goes to brush his teeth.

"Nothing," Terence says when he finds Claude, Eddie, and Novia waiting for him near the front doors after school as the buses are loading.

"Not even one text?" Claude says. "I don't get it."

"I do," Novia says. "My brother is a jerk."

"That's true," Eddie says, "but what does that have to do with anything?"

"He probably spread the word at the high school that no one should answer the flyer," Novia says.

"Seriously?" Terence says, irritated.

"I wouldn't put it past him," Novia says. "Gotta catch my bus. Don't want to miss my lesson today."

"We should go too," Eddie says, grabbing Terence's arm.

"And I have hockey practice," Claude says. "But don't worry. Someone will want to join. Meanwhile, we can keep having rehearsals as a quartet."

"True," Terence concedes, and he lets Eddie pull him to the bus.

When he gets home, Dad's out. "Probably at the doctor again," he mutters to himself.

But the fridge is restocked, and the dishes are clean, and the laundry is done. Maybe Dad's doing the right thing getting some help.

Still, Terence can't help feeling a little resentful that

Dad might just be *done* mourning. Terence will never be done.

He pulls the tub of peanut butter from the fridge and opens a new pack of Oreos. The first cookie breaks when he uses it to scoop up some peanut butter. "Dang."

His phone vibrates on the table, making him jump. He grabs the phone, hopeful that a drummer has finally replied to their ad.

But nope. Just Eddie: *Anything?*

Terence rolls his eyes. He was sitting next to her on the bus literally ten minutes ago. He's about to type back a reply when the phone shakes again.

"Jeez, Eddie," he mumbles as he pulls down the notification, but it's not from her. It's from a number he doesn't recognize.

Saw your flyer. I'd like to audition. -J

Terence quickly forwards the text to the others, adding: *Anyone know who this is?*

No!

Nope.

DID YOU WRITE BACK?!

The last one's from Eddie, of course.

Terence stares at the text from J, thinking. Finally he types back, *We can come to you. Where's your kit?*

The reply comes right away: *I can travel. Have a car too. Say when and where.*

Terence sends a reply to his bandmates. *Tomorrow afternoon OK with everyone?*

Yes!

5? Can't miss hockey.

YES

So Terence replies with Claude's address, and J says it's fine: *See you then.*

"I told him 5:15," Terence says when the four bandmates are gathered in Claude's basement the next afternoon. "So we have time to talk first."

"About what?" Eddie says, sneering.

"What if he's terrible?" Terence says. "What are we looking for, anyway? Do we have a style in mind?"

"Versatility," Claude says. "If he's sixteen, he probably only plays heavy. Can he dial it back for jazz?"

"He saw the flyer," Novia points out. "If he didn't like jazz, he wouldn't be coming down here."

"He might if he's desperate to join a band," Terence points out. "I mean, I would."

Claude's mom calls down the basement steps. "Aren't you guys expecting a drummer?"

"Yeah, Mom!" Claude calls back. "Is he here?"

"Must be," she replies. "But he doesn't have drums."

Terence stands. "They're probably still in his car," he says. "Let's go help him unload."

But when he and Eddie are halfway up the steps, the drummer appears at the top and says, "Nothing to unload — Oh."

"Oh," Terence echoes.

"Oh," Eddie repeats.

Because the boy standing in the doorway at the top of the steps is none other than James, the rudest server at Paulie's Pizza.

CHAPTER NINETEEN

"So," James says, sitting on the old basement couch. No one has said anything since Claude's mom excused herself and James sat down. They've just sat there, staring at their hands, looking at James, a little confused. "I didn't know it was you three — er, four."

"Hi," Novia says.

"Hi," James says.

"You don't have any drums," Terence points out.

James pats the black hardcase on the couch beside him. It looks a bit like the sort of briefcase you always see in movies and TV shows when someone has to make a huge illicit payment in cash, except it's not handcuffed to his wrist and James is wearing skinny jeans, a hoodie, and a parka with a fur-trimmed hood instead of a black suit and dark glasses.

"Everything I need is in here," he says, "if I can plug into your PA?"

"So, what?" Eddie says. She's standing in the middle of the room, sneering down at him. "You're like Skrillex or something?"

"Not exactly," James says. "But I can program or improvise a drum track to whatever you four can play. I guarantee that."

He pulls off his parka, turns sideways on the couch, and pops open the briefcase. "Play something," he says. "And give me a few minutes to program. You'll see."

Terence shrugs and picks up his bass. Claude warms up with a few arpeggios, and Novia makes the harp sing. Eddie flips on the PA.

"Um, 'Now At Last'?" Terence says.

"Blossom Dearie," Eddie says. "Got it."

Claude plays the intro. Terence joins in. Novia listens for the changes and lays down a rich harp part. When Eddie starts singing, the whole package is lovely.

James sits focused on his open laptop as he pulls on headphones and uncovers one ear to listen to the band. After the first refrain, he unwinds a cable, crosses to the PA system at Eddie's feet, and plugs in. Then he returns to his laptop and clicks the mouse.

The speakers click and hiss as James's beat joins the band. Instantly, what had been a classic bebop sound zooms into the 21st century with the sparse electronic drum sounds, as if cool jazz and dance music had a baby.

Terence watches James click around on his laptop, his head nodding to his own beat.

He wants to hate it. He wants to tell James to get out and take his computer with him and to never darken their doorway again. He wants to say, *And we won't be eating at Paulie's anymore, either!*

But he can't. Because it sounds amazing. And looking around at his bandmates' faces, he sees they feel the same way. Eddie looks irritated and delighted at the same time — maybe irritated that she's delighted.

When the song's over, even James looks pleasantly surprised. "Wow," he says.

"Yeah," Novia says.

"That was really, really cool," Eddie admits, dropping onto the old recliner in the corner. It creaks as she leans back and kicks out her feet.

"I gotta admit," James says. "I didn't think you guys would sound very good. But you do. You're a talented bunch of kids."

"Hey," Novia says. "We're not *kids* any more than you are."

"I don't know," James says. "I have a job. And a car."

Novia frowns at him.

"Look, the point is," James says, "your sound is pretty classic and you all have skills. I think I can add something fresh, though."

"Yeah, I agree," Terence says. "So you'll join?"

James looks at him like he's crazy. "Are you kidding?" he says. "Obviously."

Terence smiles and sighs. "All right," he says. "I think this band is finally complete."

Claude plays a celebratory run up the piano. "Now we just need a name."

"Oh, I've got that covered," James says. "The James Gang. I've been saving it."

"Excuse me?" Eddie says, putting a fist on a hip.

"You've been saving it," Terence says, laughing, "but you never googled it. There already was a James Gang."

"What?" James says. "Really?"

Terence nods. "Listen to the classic rock station once in a while," he says. "Anyway, we're not naming the band after you."

Eddie opens her mouth to say something, but Terence keeps going, cutting her off.

"Not after me, either," he says. "Don't worry."

"Let's do a few more," Claude says, and then adds, leaning around the piano to see James on the couch, "unless you have to get to your job in your car?"

"Ha." James laughs. "I got the night off. I can play as late as you guys can, unless you're bedtimes are really early?"

Eddie throws a little pillow across the room and it hits James in the face.

Novia plucks her harp — the opening of Joanna Newsom's "The Book of Right On."

"Ah!" Eddie says, leaping up from her chair. "I knew it. I can totally sing this."

"It's pretty high," Novia says over her own staccato playing.

"I'll bring it down an octave," Eddie says. "It'll sound good."

And she starts, and it does sound good — rich and a little creepy. James obviously knows the song, because he joins in with his electronic beats right away. It's not the frenetic hip-hop beat the Roots used when they sampled the same song. It's half the speed, sparse and laid back.

Terence follows the musical cues, and his bass line is barely there. When Claude joins in, his piano part contributes some hushed background tones. Add it all up, and the sound was beyond anything Terence thought this band could be.

The new band plays till after eight, when Claude's mom finally makes them stop and reminds them all they have homework they should probably being doing. Even James's eyes go wide at that.

They break for the night and go their separate ways. Eddie's mom gives Terence a ride home again, this time without the difficult, heavy condolences.

But when Terence unlocks the door to the rental house and steps inside, he finds Dad.

And it's not the new dad — the one in khakis and a sweater and a smile. This is the dad he's known for the last six months, on his back on the couch, the TV on and his eyes closed.

Terence pulls the blanket from the back of the couch and lays it over his father and kisses his cheek.

"Night, Dad," Terence says. "See you in the morning."

CHAPTER TWENTY

"Did you get the email from James?" Eddie says as she slides into the empty spot next to Terence on the bus on Monday morning.

Terence nods. "Sounds really good."

James — the new "drummer" and their waiter at Paulie's — managed to get a recording of two songs at his audition and their first practice together the night before. He set up a couple of microphones and connected his laptop to the PA output.

"We have a demo, Terence," Eddie says, leaning back in her seat like she just finished a great meal.

"They sound good," Terence says. "But we should get them sounding perfect before we play it for people."

"I already played it for Luke," she says. "And my mom and dad."

"Well, that's fine," Terence says.

"And everyone at the bus stop," Eddie says.

"Oh."

"And I put it on my YouTube channel."

"What?!" Terence says, sitting bolt upright.

"Kidding," Eddie says. "Relax. I don't have a YouTube channel."

"Whew," Terence says, and then adds, "We should probably start one."

Eddies laughs as the bus pulls up to the curb in front of Franklin Middle and squeaks to a stop.

It's a good day at school. Terence sees Novia in advisory, and they secretly listen to the demo together, sharing earbuds in the back of the classroom.

He sees Claude in the halls and they give each other a thumbs-up. "Demo sounds sick, T!" Claude says.

He eats lunch with Eddie and her brother. Even Luke admits the songs sound good.

When he climbs on the bus at the end of the day, Eddie has a seat saved for him. His phone shakes in his pocket. It's a group text from James to the band: *Can't stop listening to our songs!*

When he walks from the bus stop to his house along

Maybe It's Not So Bad Living Here After All Lane, he's feeling pretty good. But when he opens the door, there's Dad, lying on the couch in his pajama pants and a ragged T-shirt.

"You awake?" Terence says as he drops his book bag next to the couch in the small living room.

The TV is on, and Dad's eyes are open but glazed. He's staring at the TV, but he doesn't seem to really see it.

"Dad?" Terence sits on the arm of the couch near Dad's feet.

"Hi, kid," Dad says in a distant voice. He's as far away as ever, as if the last couple of weeks of relative happiness never happened.

Maybe he's even worse.

"Did you see Dr. Hyacinth today?" Terence says.

Dad pulls his red and wet eyes from the TV to look at Terence. "No," he says. "I'm not going to see her anymore."

"Why not?"

Dad forces himself to sit up. "I'm pretty depressed, Terence."

"Of course you are," Terence says. "So am I."

"You're doing well, though," Dad says. He sounds like he might cry.

Terence's phone shakes in his pocket.

"See that?" Dad says. "You just got a text. Probably from that girl with a boy's name."

"Eddie," Terence confirms.

Dad shakes his head and lets his head fall back to look at the ceiling. "You've got friends. You're doing so well at your new school. And I still feel terrible, every day about everything."

"I do too," Terence says. He's not sure it's true, but it's sometimes true.

Dad pulls Terence by the arm till he's sitting next to him. "I wanted Dr. Hyacinth to fix me," Dad says. "I thought it'd be like getting antibiotics for an infection. Like, she'd give me a pill, and I'd feel all better. I wouldn't be sad anymore."

"People take pills for depression."

"That's not how Dr. Hyacinth sees it," Dad says. "She says I'm not depressed. She says I'm mourning, and that's not a clinical condition. She recommended talk therapy, not medication."

"Makes sense," Terence says.

"I know," Dad says nodding. "It just sounds a whole lot harder."

The TV is playing an old *X-Files* episode. Terence and Dad sit together and watch till the commercial break.

Terence pulls out his phone. The text is from Eddie, but he doesn't read it. Instead he opens his music player.

"Listen to this, Dad," he says, and he taps play on their version of "Now At Last."

It opens with just Claude's piano and Eddie's vocals.

Dad smiles a tiny bit as he stares down at the phone in Terence's hand: just that blank CD art and the little blue bar at the bottom crawling from left to right.

The harps come in with Terence's bass, followed closely by James's slow and sparse beat, and Dad actually flinches in surprise.

"This is really nice," he says. "It's not Billie Holiday, obviously. A remix of her, maybe?"

Terence smiles and shakes his head.

"No, she never sang this, I bet, " Dad says. "Did you make this?"

"Sort of," Terence says as Novia takes a short harp solo after the second refrain. "That's me on bass."

Dad's eyes go wide, and he flashes his proud smile. Terence hasn't seen it in a while.

"No kidding?" Dad says. "You know this is one of my favorite songs. Mom loved it."

"I know."

"Makes it kind of bittersweet right now," Dad admits. "So who's singing?"

"That's Eddie," Terence says.

"What?" Dad says, stunned. "So this is your new band?"

Terence nods.

"Don't play it for Polly," Dad says. "This girl's better."

"Dad," Terence says, shaking his head.

They listen to the rest of the track and the next one, Dad with an arm around Terence's shoulders the whole time, hardly speaking except to say things like, "Amazing," and "Ooh, that was nice."

When the songs are done, Dad gives Terence an extra squeeze, turns off the TV, and stands up. "Mac and cheese tonight?" he says.

They go to the kitchen together to make supper.

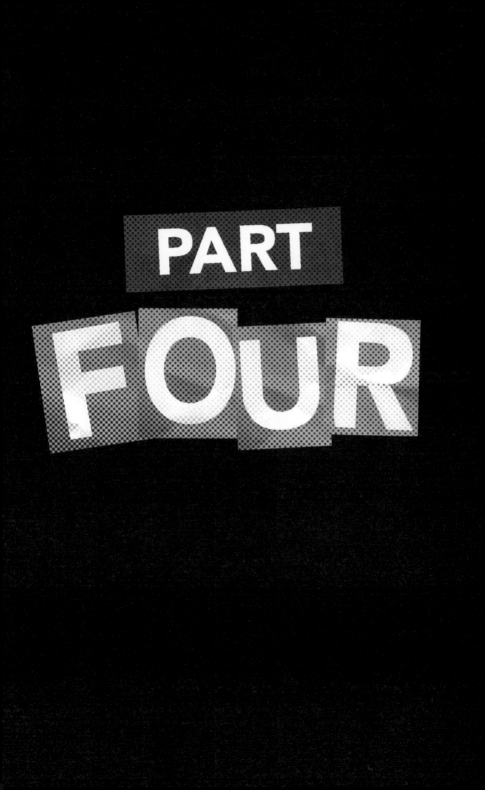

PART

FOUR

CHAPTER TWENTY-ONE

It's Saturday afternoon and early March in Minneapolis. Outside, the air is crisp and dry, the sky as clear blue and beautiful as any perfect summer day, but the trees are bare, and the lawns are covered in layered blankets of snow.

Mounds of frozen slush stained gray by car exhaust, street salt, and sand line the sidewalks and trap the odd car and bicycle whose owner didn't move them in time for the plows.

But in the basement of the Viateur home — where the slim windows set high in the walls have been covered by soundproof foam and thick black curtains — you'd never know it. It's warm and dim, lit only by a pair of lamps in opposite corners and a string of amber Christmas lights that run along the crown molding.

The four members of the still unnamed new band gathered twenty minutes ago, and have already played through three songs from Terence's set.

"They sound really good," he says as he clicks on his bass's tuning pedal and checks the open A string.

"Yeah," says Eddie. "I'm so glad we got a drummer!"

"It would be nice if James were on time," says Novia as she plucks a syncopated line that bounces between the bass and treble strings of her instrument. "I mean, now and then."

Claude plays a high trill on the keys. "If he brings pizza to every practice, he can be late to every practice."

As if on cue, the doorbell rings upstairs and they hear Ms. Viateur's hurried footsteps across the first floor. A moment later, James is hurrying down the basement steps, his heavy-duty laptop case under one arm and a pizza in his hands.

"Check this out," he says, and he drops the pizza in the center of the basement floor and tosses his laptop onto the couch next to the half-reclined Eddie.

"Pineapple?" Eddie asks, bored-sounding and bored-looking.

"What?" James says as he pulls a folded paper from his back pocket. "Oh, the pizza. No. Peppers. Messed-up order so they let me take it. It's probably cold. But look at this."

He unfolds the paper and drops it on top of the pizza box. Claude, who was already up to get a slice of pizza, kneels beside the box. Eddie leans off the couch a little. Terence keeps his bass around his neck and shoulders and leans between them. He recognizes the logo at the top of the flyer at once.

"What is it?" Novia says.

Terence reads aloud: "The Wellstone Music Battle of the KID Bands. May fourteenth. All band members must be sixteen or younger."

"That's us," Novia says.

Terence nods as Eddie picks up the paper and leans back on the couch with it. Claude takes the opportunity to open the pizza box and take a slice.

"First place prize a gift certificate for ten *thousand* dollars, split among the band members," Eddie says, reading from the paper, "and recording time, *and* a slot on a store-sponsored and -produced compilation."

"Wow," Terence says.

"That's only two thousand for each of us," Novia points out.

"Only?" Eddie says. "I'll take it."

Terence nods again. "Think we can be ready in time?" he says. "It's only two months away. I'd been meaning to mention it, but I wasn't sure everyone would be into the idea."

"Very into it," Claude says with his mouth full.

"Man, I'm ready *now*," Eddie says as she folds the paper into an airplane.

"I don't know," Terence says. "I remember this battle from last year. My band didn't even enter — since my mom was sick. But I heard the competition was tough."

"Absolutely," James says, sitting down and opening his laptop. "I've gone to the last three battles. Bands come from all over the state. It's no joke. And you know who won last year."

Claude shakes his head.

Terence says it almost solemnly: "Time Stereo."

"Yup," James says. "Look at them now."

"Come on," Eddie says as James pulls his cables across her lap to reach the PA. "You're telling me Time Stereo are only big today because they won some dumb battle of the bands? Please."

"Why not?" Novia says.

"Because their YouTube channel has like three million subscribers?" Eddie says. "They didn't get all of them from a battle of the bands sponsored by a Podunk music store."

"Maybe," James says, "but it's a good enough endorsement for me."

"Me too," Claude says as he takes his second slice.

Eddie tosses her paper airplane across the room so it hits Terence in the face.

"Hey!" he says.

"You know what we need, though," she says, "if we're going to sign up for this battle?"

"Five bucks each for the entry fee," James says.

Eddie kicks him. "I mean," she says, "what we need is a name."

"And quick," James says. "Entrance deadline is next Friday."

"OK," Terence says. "So we have a few days to think about it. Anyone have any ideas?"

No one says anything.

Terence sighs. "And I guess we'll need a few days."

CHAPTER TWENTY-TWO

On Monday morning, Terence climbs off his bus with Eddie at his heels. They've ridden the bus together most mornings since Terence changed schools in January, only missing a morning here and there when Terence couldn't bear to see her, right after she found out his mom had died.

This morning, they part in the front hall with a fist bump. Eddie slips in earbuds and says, "Hot new tracks."

Terence knows she's listening to their band — the "demo" songs James recorded. They're not exactly professional recordings, but despite being the most obnoxious server at Paulie's, the guy knows a thing or two about production.

At his audition, he recorded two of the songs they played together. On Saturday — after deciding to enter the battle of the bands and eating some pizza — he recorded four more songs and emailed them to his middle school bandmates.

"They're really rough, OK?" Terence says, holding on to Eddie's hand before she hurries off to her advisory class. "Don't play them for anyone."

"I know, I know," she says, pulling her hand away. "Don't worry about it, OK?"

Terence smirks at her, and she smiles at him.

"Don't worry so much!" she says, and then she waves as she walks fast down the front hall to her locker.

"They sound *good*," Novia says. She sits next to Terence in advisory.

"I know," Terence says. He's excited about how good the demo tracks sound, but he wants them to be perfect. "Did you . . . did you play them for anyone?"

She shakes her head. "Just my sister and brother this morning," she says. Her sister is in elementary school and her brother is a high school senior. "Rosa danced all over the living room. Santino said it was garbage and turned off the speakers on Mom and Dad's computer."

"How nice." Terence scratches his pen across the back of his spiral notebook, absentmindedly trying to come up with band names. He hasn't had a single idea yet.

Novia shrugs. "Sonny's a moron. He doesn't like anything I like just out of spite. His opinion is invalid."

"And Rosa?" Terence asks.

"She's nine," Novia admits with a shrug. "If it's music, she dances to it."

The bell rings to end advisory, and they have a few minutes before first hour starts. Most of them stay in the same room, though, so no one gets up. They just start talking to each other in slightly louder voices.

One of the few kids whose advisory is in a different classroom shows up and drops into the desk in front of Novia. "No," she says — a nickname, not a negative, "those songs you sent me this morning are so good."

"Thanks," Novia says, glancing at Terence as her face goes red. "I guess I sent it to Gina too. Do you know Gina?"

"No," Terence says, glaring at both the girls. "Nice to meet you."

"You too," she says. "Have you heard it?"

"Um, yes," Terence says.

"Terence is in the band with me!" Novia explains.

Gina doesn't seem especially impressed by that, and the buzzer rings to start first hour. Gina waves goodbye as she hurries to her spot closer to the front of the room.

"So you didn't just play it for your sister and brother," Terence says quietly.

"Yes, I did!" Novia insists quietly. "I didn't play it for Gina. I just *sent* it to her. She's been my best friend since like kindergarten, Terence."

"Did you *send* it to anyone else?"

Novia shakes her head, a tight smile on her lips. "I mean, a few people."

"No."

"I'm sorry," she whispers. "I'm proud of it, you know?"

How can Terence be mad? He's proud of it too, and even if the production isn't ideal, the songs sound pretty great. "Yeah, I know," he says. "Don't worry about it. Maybe everyone will like it."

At lunch, Terence finds Eddie at their usual spot. Unusually, though, she isn't alone. Even more unusually, the people surrounding her chair at their table are not Luke and Claude, or even Novia, or one of Eddie's pre-band friends he sees around sometimes.

These are essentially strangers. He recognizes two of them from his own class schedule, but the rest are only vaguely familiar from the halls. A few seem to be in seventh or even sixth grade.

And whoever they are, they seem to adore Eddie.

"Um, hi," Terence says as he walks up to the gaggle of admirers surrounding his singer.

Eddie looks up and jumps to her feet, almost knocking her chair over. "Terry!" she says, and quickly, "I mean Terence. Isn't this *amazing?*"

"What is *this*, exactly?" Terence says, dropping his bag on the chair next to Eddie.

"They all love our band!" Eddie says.

Terence opens his mouth to reply but nothing comes out. He only stares dumbly at the gang of onlookers, all of them exclaiming how *amazing* the demo songs are, what an *amazing* singer Eddie is, and how could they have gone to school with her and not known how *amazing* she is.

"Come on," Eddie says, grabbing Terence by the elbow and pulling him to the snack-bar line. Their "new fans" stay behind, talking among themselves, presumably about how amazing Eddie is. "Can you believe it?"

Terence, practically gaping at the crowd back at their table as he steps into the snack bar, says, "Not really."

Just then, Novia sprints into the snack bar with them. "You guys," she says, almost squealing with excitement.

"Right?" Eddie says, and the two girls throw their arms around each other in celebration.

"How many people did you send the songs to?" Terence says, trying to get their attention.

Eddie shrugs and holds Novia in a half embrace. "Maybe ten?"

"Easily ten," Novia says. "And Gina sent it to a few people, she says. I don't know."

Terence leans against the refrigerated drinks case.

"Off the glass!" shouts the man behind the counter.

"Sorry," Terence says, standing up straight again.

"Don't look some glum," Eddie says, poking Terence in the belly. "Everyone likes it! This is *amazing* news."

"I don't know . . . ," Terence says.

"What's not to know?" Novia says. "Do you know how many compliments I got just walking to the cafeteria from my last class?"

Terence would like to explain — how he counted on being invisible at this school, how he didn't want to make waves or even ripples, how he hoped to escape into the sea of the huge high school in the fall as anonymous as possible.

These two would never understand.

"I'm buying you a bagel, T-man!" Eddie says as she bounds to the counter to order.

"T-man?" he mutters, Novia laughing beside him. His phone vibrates in his pocket at the same moment

Novia's chirps a harp solo of Bach's "Jesu, Joy of Man's Desiring," and Eddie's belts out the opening pogo sound of Bikini Kill's "Rebel Girl."

Terence pulls out his phone as the girls do the same. "It's from James," he says, and reads to himself: *Um guys what DID YOU DO???*

"Uh-oh," Novia says, her eyes going wide.

"What?" Terence says as Eddie huddles up with them. "What is he talking about?"

Novia shakes her head. "It can't be," she whispers, and at the same moment Claude comes into the snack bar.

"Yo," he says, strutting up to the counter. He orders a chicken griller with fruit salad, and then says over his shoulder to his bandmates. "Get that text from James?"

They all nod.

"According to Scotty's big sister," Claude says, "who is in eleventh, our demo is right at this moment being played over the school-wide PA at East High."

Terence's phone slips from his hand and drops to the dull gold and red tile floor. So much for anonymity.

CHAPTER TWENTY-THREE

"I don't see what the big deal is," Claude says, taking a huge bite of his chicken sandwich.

Their gaggles of fans have dispersed, leaving the four band members to enjoy their lunches in relative peace.

Inside, though, Terence is anything but peaceful.

"How?" he says. "How could this happen?"

"It's Sonny," Novia says. "It has to be."

"Why?" Terence says.

"Well," Novia drawls, pushing the last piece of fruit, "he said he hated it. So either he lied and wanted to spread it all over the high school, or he really thought it was terrible and wanted to embarrass us."

Claude taps his nose.

Novia sticks her tongue out at him. "Anyway," she says, "his girlfriend works in the main office one hour every day."

"And she uses the PA system?" Terence says.

"She does the announcements," Novia says, shrugging. "I think."

"You know," Eddie breaks in, "that's not a bad name for a band."

"What? The Announcements?" Terence asks. "Eh, I'm not loving it."

"No." Eddie laughs. "Public Address System."

"I don't hate it," says Claude.

"Me either," Novia agrees.

"Could be a little — I don't know — *jazzier*?" says Terence, unimpressed.

"What about PA System?" Eddie offers. "Maybe PA Quintet."

"Maybe," Terence echoes.

"That means yes," says Eddie with a smile.

Just then, all their phones chime again. Only Claude doesn't flinch. He just takes another huge bite of his chicken sandwich.

So. Everyone loves it. But Lucy's in trouble.

"That's Sonny's girlfriend," Novia says.

"I thought her name was Sandra," Claude says, furrowing his brow.

Novia shakes her head. "They broke up after Christmas."

"Huh."

"Um, guys?" Eddie says, her huge grin lit up like a string of lights across her face. "Who cares about Santino's love life? Literally everyone loves our band. We've got the battle of the bands in the bag."

"Whoa, wait, wait," Terence says. "First of all, no we don't. Remember what James said. There'll be bands from all over the state. There might be bands from Hart Arts too."

"Ooh," Novia says. "I'm *so* scared."

Eddie and Claude laugh.

"Fine, laugh," Terence says. "But I promise there will be serious competition."

"It's not like we're gonna stop practicing," Eddie points out as she stands up to bus her tray. "Stop worrying, worrier."

"I can't help it," Terence says, crossing his arms.

"No kidding," Claude says, elbowing him lightly and then stealing a chunk of his bagel.

Terence grunts. "I'm not hungry anyway."

The newly named PA Quintet does keep up rehearsals of course, twice during the week and then again on Saturday afternoon.

James manages to make it almost on time.

"No pizza, though," Claude points out.

"Can't have your pizza and eat it too," James quips.

The Saturday afternoon is a full run-through of all the songs they've been learning together. They're still mostly tunes Terence performed with the Kato Quintet back at Hart, but a few wouldn't work with this lineup. Of course, thanks to Novia's and Eddie's influence on the sound, he added a few songs too.

"Feeling any better?" Eddie says as the band packs up.

Terence has begun leaving his bass in the Viateurs' house, so today — with mid-March offering up the first spring-like day in months — he biked to practice.

"Yeah, I guess," he says. "We sound good. Should be ready for the battle in seven weeks."

"That's the spirit," James says when he's halfway up the stairs, his laptop dangling from one hand. "See you dorks next week."

Novia zips up her harp's bag and Claude rises from the piano to help her bring it up the basement steps. She can't leave it here because she still sees her private harp teacher twice a week at her house.

"You leaving too?" Terence says.

Eddie shakes her head and drops onto the old, ratty couch. "My mom won't be here for another twenty minutes." She pulls the Viateur's old acoustic guitar out from under the couch and waggles her eyebrows. "I'll amuse myself."

"OK," Terence says. "See ya. Good job today."

"Thanks, boss," she says, saluting with the guitar in her lap.

Terence rolls his eyes and heads upstairs. He says goodbye to Claude and Novia, who are out front loading the harp into Novia's dad's car.

At his bike, he digs into his pocket, finds the key to his bike lock, and realizes he left his phone in the basement. "Dang it."

Novia's car skids away from the curb and Claude goes back inside. Terence jogs to follow him and rings the bell.

"Oh, Terence," says Ms. Viateur. "Forget something?"

"Phone," Terence says.

Claude's mom steps aside. "Down you go, then," she says.

Terence hurries to the basement steps and freezes at the top. He expected to find Eddie and Claude, joking or laughing or even playing music together, but Claude is in the kitchen pouring himself a bowl of cereal. From the top of the basement steps, though, he can hear Eddie.

She's playing one of her own again, and her guitar playing is a bit better this time. Her voice is too. Maybe that's his imagination. He's been hanging out with her a lot, after all, and has gotten to like her.

As a friend.

Terence stands there, just listening to her voice and her words and the melody she's written.

"My dude," Claude says, coming up behind him, his mouth full of something crunchy and smelling of artificial flavors and sugar. "What are you doing?"

"Nothing!" Terence says, jumping. "I forgot my phone."

"OK," Claude says, heading back to the kitchen. "Go get it then."

Downstairs, Eddie stops playing. Terence hurries into the basement.

"Hello," Eddie says, the guitar on her lap.

"Forgot my phone," Terence says.

"I know," Eddie says. "It's right there." She nods toward the arm of the couch.

"Thanks," Terence says, scooping it up. "Well, bye again."

He bikes home pedaling furiously, his heart pounding maybe not just from the exertion.

CHAPTER TWENTY-FOUR

On Sunday morning, Dad is up and dressed and sipping coffee at the kitchen table, scrolling through his phone, when Terence comes in, still groggy with sleep.

"Kiddo," Dad says. "Gotta hit the mall today."

"What?" Terence says, dropping into the seat across from Dad. "Why?"

Terence can't remember the last time his dad went to the mall, never mind willingly.

"I need work clothes," Dad says, laying his phone down on the table.

"You work at home," Terence says, and adds in his mind, *Or you used to.*

Dad's freelance graphic design and illustration work

has been pretty sparse the last few months. Terence hoped as Dad worked through his depression, he'd start working more again. Maybe this is a good sign.

"Well," Dad says, picking up his phone again and setting it right down, "I have a job interview on Tuesday morning."

"Seriously?" Terence says. "For, like, an office job?"

"Is that so far-fetched?" Dad says, as if he's offended.

"It's been a while," Terence says.

"Eight years," Dad says. "Not so long."

"I don't know, Dad," Terence says. "A lot's changed. Have you heard of the 'Internet'?"

"You're hilarious," Dad says and takes a long drink of his coffee. "Now get dressed. I want to be there before it gets crowded."

Terence splits off from his dad at the first discount-designer clothing store and heads to the southeast corner of the mall — the weird part. It's where the dollar store is and the place that only sells items made of alpaca fur, and Keys, Strings, Skins, and More, the only musical instrument store in the mall. It doesn't get a lot of traffic, but they still let anyone who comes by play the electric piano near the entrance.

Terence used to spend a lot of time here when his mom and dad took him to the mall when he was little.

He even got to know the manager, Hillary. Today, though, is Sunday, and Hillary isn't working.

Terence sits on the bench at the electric piano, switches it to church organ, and plays the opening of "Whiter Shade of Pale."

"Ooh, haven't heard anyone play *that* before," says a very familiar and snarky voice.

Terence looks up from the keys, and there's Polly Winger.

Terence's fingers slip from the keys into his lap.

"Hi, Terence." She opens her arms for a hug.

"Polly," Terence says, clumsily standing up and putting one arm around her. "Hi."

"I haven't talked to you in so long," Polly says. "How are you doing?" She asks in that particular way — with sadness in her voice and that crease between her eyebrows — so he knows what she means. *Are you still sad that your mom died?*

As if he'll ever stop.

"I'm OK," he says with a shrug. "Um, how's everyone at Hart?"

"You know, same as always." Polly rolls her eyes. "Of course we had to change the name of the quintet and bring in Noel from ninth to play bass for you."

"Oh," Terence says, looking at his feet. "Yeah, I started a new band, actually."

Polly's eyes go wide. "Wow, really?" she says. "I didn't know they even had a music program at Franklin."

"Yeah, well," Terence says, "it's not very good. But there are a handful of talented kids."

"Bet your singer isn't as good as me, though, huh," Polly says, tossing a joking elbow at him.

Terence feels his face go hot.

"Aw, don't worry," Polly says, letting him off the hook. "I'm sure the new singer is wonderful too. Is it another jazz combo?"

Terence opens his mouth to answer and remembers the phone in his pocket. He grins as he pulls it out and clicks open the tracks James recorded. "Sort of," he says. "Listen."

Polly looks doubtful as she takes his phone and puts the speaker to her ear. "She *is* good," she says when Eddie's vocals come in. "Tone's a bit thin."

"You're listening to her on a phone," Terence says. "Once you hear it with headph—"

"Is that . . . ," Polly says, cutting him off. "Is that *electronic drums?*"

"Yeah," Terence says. "Sounds good, right?"

She shrugs. Before the song is over, she hands him the phone back. "It sounds pretty good."

"Just *pretty* good?" Terence says, getting a little irritated with Polly's Hart Arts snobbery. He goes on before he can stop himself. "Everyone at Franklin loves it."

Polly grins wickedly. "Mmhm," she says. "A student body who thinks jazz is a basketball team and classical music begins and ends with Pachelbel's Canon in D."

Terence is fuming. He shoves his phone into his pocket, prepared to storm off, but instead he opens his big mouth one more time. "Yeah, well we'll be playing the battle of the bands in May. We'll see what the judges think."

Polly's grin vanishes as she juts out her lower jaw and scowls. "*You're* entering?" she says. "You can't. *We're* entering."

"So?"

"So?!" Polly says. "Terence, we used to be your best friends. You're going to compete against us now?"

"Key words being 'used to,'" Terence spits.

"Ha!" Polly says. "Like you've been Mister In-Touch since you left."

"Whatever," Terence says. *At least I have an excuse.*

"Yeah, whatever to you," Polly says. "See at the battle, public-school boy."

With that, she flips her hair and walks away. Terence watches her till she sits with a group of her friends who'd been watching the whole thing from the coffee shop at the far end of the corridor.

"Thought I'd find you here," says Dad as he walks up behind him. "Was that Polly Winger?"

"Yeah," Terence says, still staring at his former friend. "Are you done shopping?"

"Yup," Dad says. "Wanna get some lunch in the food court? Something fast and fried and greasy?"

"I'm not hungry," Terence says, and without waiting for Dad, walks fast toward the parking ramp.

CHAPTER TWENTY-FIVE

As Minneapolis thaws completely, the PA Quintet meets more and more often. Hockey season ends, so Claude is available for practice practically every day. Novia still has her harp lesson, and James still has to work the dinner shift at Paulie's now and then, but even then the rest of the band often gets together to run through their set list minus one.

It's dinnertime one Saturday at the beginning of May, and the PA Quintet has been practicing most of the day. Now they lounge around in the Viateurs' media room. Ms. V loaded up two trays of pizza rolls, set out cut veggies and ranch dip, and stocked the mini-fridge with every drink she imagined the band would like.

Terence sits on the floor with his legs under the central coffee table and his back against Eddie's legs, who lounges in the cushy gaming chair.

"I'm telling you," James says. "We have the battle on lock. We sound sick."

"Sick," Novia says, nodding, just before she chomps a celery stick.

Terence laughs and pops a pizza roll in his mouth — and immediately regrets it. The hot, molten core explodes into his mouth, leaving him gasping. He reaches for his juice pouch. Empty.

Eddie squeals and leans across him, grabs her own pouch, and shoves it into his hand.

Terence takes a long pull — it's peach flavor and he hates peach, but it doesn't matter. It's nearly empty when he puts it down on the coffee table. "Thanks," he says, breathless.

"You," Claude says, grabbing a handful of pizza rolls, "are an amateur." He pops the pizza rolls into his mouth one after another and chews slowly with his mouth open, gasping in breaths of cool air.

"See," he says, "you have to cool the sauce and cheese as you go. And you don't let them burst. You make them leak slowly."

"Sounds delicious," Eddie says.

"Oh, it is," Claude says as he finishes his mouthful

and wipes his mouth with the back of his hand. "It is."

"Claude!" his mom snaps as she happens past the doorway. "Napkin!"

"Sorry, Mom!" Claude says, grabbing a paper napkin from the stack next to the veggies plate. "I swear, she has a sixth sense."

Everyone laughs. It's hard to be sure whether they're laughing with Claude or at him, but he doesn't seem to care either way. Lounging there on the floor with Eddie cracking up behind him, Novia across from him, and Claude and James on the couch, Terence feels a warmth that he hasn't felt in a long time.

He knows what it is, of course, but maybe if he doesn't say it — if no one says anything about it — having a new group of friends won't be so bad.

Terence is sitting there, his mind wandering like that, a smile on his face, when Eddie squeezes his shoulder and says something.

"Hm?" he says, looking up at her and finding her upside-down face looking back at him. She's not laughing now, though. She's not even smiling.

"Oh," Claude says from the couch, and he's not laughing anymore either.

What happened? Terence wonders.

"I'm really sorry," Claude says, leaning forward, his elbows on his knees. "I didn't know."

"Yeah, me either," James says. "Man, that sucks."

Terence looks across the table at Novia, whose eyes are full with tears. She doesn't say anything. She doesn't have to. It's obvious what's happened.

Terence stands up. "See?" he snaps, turning to face Eddie. "See what happens?"

"What?" Eddie says, reaching for him. "What do—"

Terence dodges, almost tripping over the coffee table, sending the platter of pizza rolls across the floor. The little puffs of orange pastry scatter like mice: under furniture, into corners, out of sight.

"No," Terence says. "This is why I didn't want friends, don't you get it? Don't you see what happens? It's contagious. It's like a *stink* I can't wash off, and now all of them know about it. They all can smell it now."

Eddie stands. "Terence, I—"

"No!" he snaps again, backing away. "I'm leaving now. No more friends. No more hanging out. No more band. It's over. Goodbye."

Terence turns his back on the Public Address Quintet, walks out of the Viateurs' house, slams the door behind him, and bikes home fast enough so the wind will dry the tears on his face.

CHAPTER TWENTY-SIX

The first two weeks of May should have been good ones.

Dad got that job, and he started the following Monday. He's getting up every morning as early as Terence. He's shaving and dressing and focusing on work. He's coming home tired but energized, smiling some days and with stories over dinner about the new job.

In fact, Dad is acting a little like Terence probably was when he was meeting new people he liked and enjoying band rehearsal.

So the first two weeks of May *should* have been and *could* have been good ones. But instead Terence spends them mostly alone. He ignores loads of texts from the members of the former PA Quintet.

From James, to the group: *So we can just assume T's meltdown is forgiven and everything's cool and practice Tuesday afternoon right?*

From Claude, to the group: *T we all promise never to mention it again and you don't smell.*

From Novia, to Terence: *I'm sorry Terence. Please come out of hiding,* which is almost amusing because she was sitting right next to him in advisory when she sent that one.

And from Eddie, to Terence and to the group, dozens of texts, apologizing to him, scolding him, lecturing him on friendship.

Terence ignores them all, deletes them from his phone, and refuses to make eye contact in the halls and in classes. At lunch, he avoids the snack bar, eats quickly, and hides out in the media center.

But even though they only met several months ago, Eddie knows Terence well enough. It's Friday lunchtime on May 13, and Terence is sitting at the last table in the media center with his head down when someone sits across from him.

Terence doesn't look up. People share the big tables in the media center all the time. It could be anyone.

Of course it's not. Out of the corner of his eye he

sees the ragged cuffs of a red plaid shirt and dark hands folded together. On one hand is a gold ring with a green gem, the kind you can buy for fifty cents from one of those machines in front of the grocery store.

It's Eddie.

"Terence," she whispers, and her voice is not mad, not exactly. But it has the tone of someone who's about ready to give up on him. "I cannot possibly understand what you've been going through."

Terence doesn't look up. He clenches his jaw, wishing she'd stop talking, but also not wanting her to leave.

"If I lost my mom . . . ," she says. "I don't even know what I'd do. I'm sure I'd lash out. A lot. I'd probably flip over this table and punch someone in the face."

Terence thinks about himself flipping the table and almost laughs as his eyes fill with tears.

"But I do know a few things," she says. "I know that I'm your friend. And Claude is, and Novia." After a beat, she adds, "I don't know about James."

Terence laughs and covers it with a sniff.

"And I know that your life *will* continue," she goes on, "whether you choose to live it or not."

Terence still says nothing. Tears drop from his eyes onto the hand he's using as a pillow.

"Your friends would like to live it with you," she says, "with or without the band."

After a few moments, she pushes back her chair and stands up.

Terence lifts his head and watches her leave the media center.

"Was that Eddie Carson?" says a sixth-grade boy, walking up to his table, his awe-filled eyes on the closing media center doors.

Terence nods.

"Isn't she amazing?" the boy says. "Her band is my favorite ever." He's practically swooning as he walks off.

CHAPTER TWENTY-SEVEN

Terence is sitting at the kitchen table doing his homework — or trying to — when Dad gets home from work.

"Hey, kiddo," Dad says, kissing the top of Terence's head. He grabs a diet soda from the fridge and sits across from him. "How's the homework going?"

Terence shakes his head. "It's not."

"Need some help?" Dad says, craning his neck to get a look at the upside-down notebook and textbook. "Ooh, polynomial equations. Might be beyond my abilities."

"No, I can do it," Terence says. "Just can't really focus."

"Something on your mind?" Dad says.

It's been a long time since Terence spoke to his dad about anything like this. In fact, even years ago, when something was bothering Terence — something at school going wrong, or some kids making fun of him — he usually went to Mom for comfort, support, or advice.

But that's not an option, so Terence takes a deep breath and lays it all out, nearly everything that's happened to him since he started at Franklin Middle School: meeting Eddie, starting the band, the competition they're supposed to play in tomorrow.

Dad knows some of it, but the details — and Terence's explosion two weeks ago — Terence hasn't shared until now.

"This is going to sound a little weird right now," Dad says, "but I'm very proud of you."

"Why?" Terence says.

"You've been through a very tough time," Dad says, "way tougher than most kids your age have to go through. You lost your mom, your school, most of your friends in the process."

"Yeah," Terence says. He feels the tears starting and blinks hard against them.

Dad takes Terence's hand on the table between them. "Here's what I think, and you can do whatever you want with this," Dad says.

Terence stares at their hands.

"Eddie sounds like a very good friend," he says. "And we know she's a terrific singer too. Your band, from what I've heard, is fantastic and you're bound to do well and at least have a very good time at the battle tomorrow — if you choose to join in. I think you might regret it if you don't."

"But there's another thing," Dad goes on, "and in a way it might be more important. Your mom loved music. She loved *your* music, and if she could be here right now . . . ," Dad trails off, and Terence looks up to find his father shaking his head slowly, a sad smile on his face. "She'd be so proud of you, Terence. *She'd* want to be there at the battle, and she'd want you to be up on that stage."

Dad squeezes Terence's hand and lets it go. He takes a drink of his pop, puts the cap on, and puts it back in the fridge. "Are you hungry?"

"Not really," Terence says, wiping his eyes.

Dad sniffs, his back to Terence, as he opens the cupboard. "Well, good. I haven't been to the grocery store since I started this new job. We're essentially out of food."

"I guess I better text Eddie," Terence says, closing his math textbook.

"That's a good idea," Dad says, "and I'll call Paulie's.

You'll get hungry when the pizza shows up, I have a feeling."

Smiling now, Terence hurries to his room and dives onto his bed, grabbing his phone. He fires off a group text first:

Can everyone get together um right now for a last-minute rehearsal. Sorry btw.

And then another to Eddie:

Thanks.

Dad makes Terence eat one slice of pizza — "Because if you don't then I'll eat it and honestly I've been stress-eating enough, thank you" — before they get in the car and zip across town to the Viateurs'.

Dad parks and switches off the car.

"Um, you're coming in?" Terence says with one foot out the door.

"Sure," Dad says. "Seems like about time I meet some of your friends' parents, right?"

"Right," Terence says, unsure. But he and Dad approach the front door together, and Ms. Viateur lets them in.

"I'm Raymond Kato," Dad says, smiling.

Ms. Viateur smiles and shakes his hand. "So glad to meet you. It's been so nice having your son over so much these past few months. I love the kids' music."

The two adults smile down at Terence.

"The talent these kids have at such a young age . . . ," Ms. Viateur says, beaming.

"It really is something," Dad says, and he smiles and musses Terence's hair.

"All right, all right," Terence says, moving farther into the house. "Is everyone down there already."

"Yup!" Ms. V says as she closes the door.

Terence hurries down the basement steps just as Ms. V says to his father, "Come in and sit for a while. Would you like some tea or something?"

"There he is!" Claude shouts from the piano, playing a fanfare.

Eddie, James, and Novia all smile up at him when he stops halfway down the steps.

"Oh good," Terence says. "Three phony smiles."

"I'm smiling too," Claude says from behind the piano.

"Four, then," Terence says, coming all the way down the steps.

Eddie meets him at the bottom with a hug. "I'm sorry too," she says quietly. "And thank *you* too."

"Me?" Terence says back. "What'd I do?"

"You started this band," she says. "You got me singing. Out loud. With other people who can hear me."

"Oh," Terence says. "Good."

Eddie nods firmly and runs back to the couch. "Now let's do this. We have a set to rehearse."

"Can we just be clear about one thing first?" James says, raising his hand. "Are we or are we not playing the battle of the bands tomorrow?"

"We are," Terence says.

The other cheer.

"That's why we have a lot of work to do tonight," Terence says.

Novia leans on her harp. "I don't know," she says. "It's only three songs, right? One per round?"

"If we last all three rounds," James points out.

"We will," Terence says, "and yes, it's just three songs, including we've never played. Well, most of us."

"Huh?" Claude says.

"You show up after two weeks gone," James says, "and just drop a new song on us? You crazy?"

"Crazy like a fox," Terence says. "I think it'll be worth it."

"So what song?" Novia asks. "Another jazz standard?"

"Zeppelin?" Claude says.

"Something current?" James says.

"Very current," Terence says, looking at Eddie. "It's not even out yet."

"What?" Eddie says. "What are you talking about, Weird Terry?"

Terence laughs. "It goes something like . . . ," he says, and then sings what he can remember of Eddie's song — the one she's been writing all spring and Terence overheard back in January and again in March.

Eddie covers her open mouth with her hand and blushes. Terence feels his face go hot too.

"What is that?" Claude says, trying to find the chords.

Novia picks at her strings, looking for right sound to match what Terence sang. "Sing it again," she says.

Terence shakes his head. "Eddie will sing," he says, and he reaches under the couch for the old acoustic. "She wrote it."

Eddie accepts the guitar and sits on the couch.

"You write songs?" James says.

"A little," Eddie admits. "I didn't know you heard me," she adds to Terence.

"Well, I did," he says, "and I'm sorry I didn't listen to you when you told me about your songs months ago."

She strums the opening chord slowly and quietly. "Are you sure about this?"

"Play it, Eddie!" Novia shouts through a smile.

"OK, OK," Eddie says. "Don't judge me too harshly." And she plays.

The PA Quintet practices the new song and the other two songs for the battle tomorrow until almost ten.

Finally, when their rendition of "Now At Last" comes to an end, Ms. V pops her head in the door at the top of the basement steps. "I think it's time to wrap up now, guys!"

"OK, Mom!" Claude says. "Pack it up!"

While Terence puts his bass away, Eddie sits on the arm of the couch beside him. "Thanks," she says quietly.

"It's a great song," Terence says.

Eddie bites her fingernail. "You think so?"

Terence nods.

"You think people will like it tomorrow?" Eddie asks.

"Definitely," Terence says.

James, with his laptop in one hand, walks by them to head upstairs. "Relax," he says. "It's a good song." He goes upstairs.

Claude and Novia carry the harp up.

"Really good, Eddie," Novia says as they pass.

Claude winks.

"See?" Terence says.

Eddie smiles. "Well, I did try to tell you on the bus that morning," she says. "Should've listened."

"There's the Eddie I know," Terence says. "And you're right." He puts his gig bag on his shoulder and together they head upstairs.

"There you are," Terence's dad says when they reach the kitchen. To everyone's surprise, he and Ms. and Mr.

Viateur have been joined by Ms. Carson and Novia's dad too.

"Uh-oh," Eddie says. "What have you old people been up to?"

"Just telling embarrassing stories," Ms. Carson says.

"Sharing baby photos," Terence's dad says.

"Stuff like that," Novia's dad says.

"See you all at the battle tomorrow?" Dad says, hopping down from his stool at the island.

The other parents agree they wouldn't miss it, and Terence and his dad head home.

In the car, Terence's eyes are heavy. He reclines the seat a little stares at the moon, which seems to follow their car as it cruises along the almost empty streets.

"Thanks, Dad," he says.

"Hm?" Dad says. "For what?"

"Driving."

CHAPTER TWENTY-EIGHT

The next morning, Terence is awake before eight. He tunes his bass, plays a few minutes, tunes it again. He changes the D and G strings, tunes again, tightens the connections under the metal panel, and plays a few more minutes.

He tunes again.

Dad opens the bedroom door and stands there yawning in his pajama pants and a tattered Iron Man T-shirt that's older than Terence.

"A little early for that, isn't it?" Dad says.

"Sorry," Terence says. "I'm so anxious for the battle."

"It doesn't start for . . . ," — he sticks his head into the room to see Terence's clock — "five more hours."

"I know," Terence says. "Still. Couldn't sleep."

Terence's phone shakes on the desk.

"Let me guess who else is awake this early on a Saturday," Dad says as he turns away, yawning again. "I'll make coffee."

The text is from Eddie: *You awake yet? CANNOT SLEEP.*

Same, Terence types back. *What time will you be down there?*

Eddie doesn't reply right away, but a few minutes later: *Ten.*

See you then, Terence replies, and then heads into the kitchen. Dad's sipping his first cup. "Think we can get to the mall a little early?" Terence asks.

Terence's dad gets a close spot and pops the hatchback.

"Are the doors even open yet?" Dad says as he climbs out.

Terence grabs his bass from the back of the car. "It's almost ten," he says. "Besides, they open early for the mall-walkers."

"Oh, right," Dad says, the two of them walking toward the mall doors. Dad nods toward the doors as an old man comes out. He's dressed in a matching tracksuit. "I suppose that'll be me in a few years."

Terence laughs. "A few, yeah."

They find Eddie and her family near the Battle of the Bands stage. It's still being set up. Luke and Mr. and Ms. Carson are sitting on a bench nearby, but Eddie is pacing in front of the half-built stage.

"Nervous?" Terence says as he walks up to her.

Terence's dad joins the Carsons on the bench.

"Very, very," Eddie says.

Terence looks over at the benches set up facing the stage. His father sits with Eddie's family in the second row. In a few hours, the benches will be full of people to watch the battle. The thought is a little overwhelming.

"Exciting too, though," Terence says out loud.

"Yeah," Eddie agrees. "I mean, of course it is. We could win."

Terence looks at her and smiles. "We totally could."

Terence's dad strolls over to them. "So if you're OK here, I'm going to walk around. Maybe get another cup of coffee. Sound good?"

"Sure," Terence says. "I'm fine."

Dad wanders off toward the food court. A moment later, Luke comes over. He punches Terence in the arm — not too hard, of course. "We're going too," he says. "See you in a few hours."

The Carsons leave, and Terence and Eddie sit on a bench in the front row to watch the stage being built.

Terence lays his bass on the bench beside him.

"So I was thinking," Terence says. "We should save your song for last."

"Good thinking," Eddie says. "That way I probably won't have to sing it."

Terence laughs and gives her a shove. "I mean I think it's our strongest song," he says, "and we should save it for the third and championship round, assuming we get that far."

Eddie stares at the stage. "You think we will?"

Terence has to think for a minute, but he says honestly, "Yeah, I think we will."

The battle begins at one, and though he knows he should eat and though Claude shows up and immediately suggests the whole band has lunch together, Terence can hardly take a bite of his sandwich.

Across from him, Eddie isn't eating either. "I can't," she says. "My tummy is doing backflips right now."

Claude leans across the table. "I'll have yours," he says, snatching it up.

Eddie slaps his hand, but he manages to take a bite anyway before putting it back.

"Everyone knows the set list?" Terence says, probably for fifth time today alone.

"Yes, Terence, yes," James says, rolling his eyes. "We

know the *three-song* set list. It's not hard to remember a *three-song* set list."

"I just wanna be sure," Terence says, slumping in his seat.

From his seat, he can look out the doorway to the sandwich shop and watch the Saturday lunchtime crowds pass by. People of all shapes and sizes and colors walk by, leisurely passing the morning and afternoon at the mall, none as nervous as he is.

One of them, though, perhaps is: in a group of old friends, her auburn hair in a bun at the top of her head and dressed in a long black dress — like she's performing in a cabaret, rather than an atrium at the mall — is Polly Winger.

She's only there for an instant — as long as it takes for a group of fourteen-year-olds, excited and nervous and full of energy — to walk by an open doorway at the mall. But it's enough.

Terence leans forward. "Guys," he says, "two things."

Everyone stops chewing to look at Terence.

"One," he says, "we have to win. My old band from Hart is here, and they're in the battle. I'd almost forgotten, but I just saw them walk by."

"For sure," James says. "They're toast."

"What's the other thing?" Novia says before slurping pop up a straw.

"Two," Terence continues, "I didn't know it was possible, but I just got even more nervous."

Terence is kneeling on the floor of a bathroom stall when someone thumps on the stall door.

"You OK in there, T?" James says. "Need me to . . . I don't know. Find your dad or something?"

Terence shakes his head and wipes his mouth. "I'm fine," he says. "Just a nervous . . . nervous . . . stomach."

"OK," James says. "Might wanna come on out of there, though. It's like five to one."

"OK," Terence says. He watches James's feet disappear under the stall door, counts to ten, checks for queasiness in his tummy, and leaves the stall. After washing his face and hands and gargling a few times, he hurries out of the bathroom.

"Finally," Eddie says. "Come *on*, guys."

Then the PA Quintet are hurrying through the mall, dodging around families and strollers and high schoolers and retirees, making their way to the atrium.

When they arrive, the stage is built, the crowd assembled, and a banner hangs over the back of the stage: *Fourteenth Annual Battle of the KID Bands*.

"Stupidest name ever," James says, shaking his head.

"Well, it's the last time you'll be able to enter," Eddie says, clapping his shoulder, "if it's any consolation."

"Oh yeah," James says, screwing up his eyebrows. "That kinda stinks."

The five stride to the side of the stage. "And this must be . . . ," says the man with the clipboard, "the Public Announcement Quintet."

"Just PA Quintet is fine too," Eddie pipes up.

"Got it," the man says, grinning at her. "Hey, I liked your demo."

"What?" James says. "You heard it?"

He nods. "My kid had it on her phone," he says.

"Does she go to Franklin Middle School?" Terence asks.

He shakes his head. "North End High," he says.

"I don't even know where that is," Eddie whispers to Novia. They both giggle, and Terence shushes them.

"Anyway, you're checked in," the clipboard man says. "In the first round, you guys are up — one, two, three . . . sixth. You're up sixth."

"Out of how many?" Claude asks.

"We have sixteen bands competing this year," clipboard man says. "Twice as many as last year. It's going to be a fun day."

"A long day too," James says.

"You can hang out in the 'green room,'" says clipboard man, putting air quotes around "green room." He nods toward a little curtained-off area behind the stage, where they can see some other kids and tables and chairs set up, along with bottles of pop and bags of chips.

Among them, Terence finds Polly Winger.

"Guys," he says, "I'll be right back."

"Is that her?" Eddie says, grabbing his arm and squinting into the green room. "The one in the cocktail dress?"

Terence nods.

"I already don't like her," Eddie says.

"Be right back," Terence says.

He walks into the green room. As soon as he steps foot inside, someone jumps up from Polly's table and holds up a hand to stop him.

"Sorry, kid," he says. "This area is for the talent only."

"Knock it off, Harrison," Terence says, for this is Harrison Engel, one-time guitar player in the Kato Quintet at Hart. "You know I'm here for the battle too."

Harrison squints at him. "Terence?" he says, as if a fog is lifting. "Terence Kato? Is that you? I — I didn't even recognize you. How long has it been? Oh, it's been too, too long. . . ."

"You're hilarious, Harrison," Terence says, dodging around the boy and stepping up to Polly's seat. "I wanted to say good luck." He puts out his hand.

Polly puts her hand in his, but not like a shake. More like a queen offering a peasant her ring to kiss. *"We,"* she says, "won't need luck. *We* are virtuosos."

Terence looks down at her — though she won't look at him at all — and he fights the anger rising in his belly. "I'm sorry I didn't stay in touch," he says quietly. "It was . . . a tough winter."

She sniffs and withdraws her hand and says softly, "I know."

"OK," Terence says. "Well, good luck."

She looks up at him finally, her eyes shaded under long lashes and loose curls across her forehead, and replies, "Good luck."

Terence returns to his bandmates just outside the green room.

"Let's watch the first five bands," Novia says. "It seems polite."

There are plenty of seats out front still. "Might help to fill the seats too," James says.

"The turnout is a little leaner than I thought it would be," Terence admits as they find an empty bench and sit down.

"Fine with me," Eddie says, rubbing her palms on her frayed jeans. "Makes me a little less nervous."

Just then, clipboard man — now without his clipboard — climbs the stage and walks to the mic.

"Ladies and gentlemen, welcome to the fourteenth annual Wellstone Music Store's — on Old Main Street at the corner of 33rd Avenue — Battle of the Kid Bands!"

The crowd claps. A few people — including Claude — hoot and holler. Passersby slow down or stop. A few even take a seat.

"We've got a whole slew of bands coming up, so let me run down quickly how this works," clipboard man says. "First round — which will begin in a few seconds — we'll hear one song from each of the sixteen bands in today's battle. The judges will eliminate *half* of those bands, and they *will* consider audience reaction.

"In round two," clipboard continues, "we'll hear a different song from the surviving eight bands. Then we'll be left with our three finalists, who will each perform a third song beginning at six this evening."

The five members of the PAQ all look at each other, hearts in their throats.

"So without further ado," says clipboard man, "let's bring out our first band, from way out in River Bluff, the Screaming Pachyderms!"

CHAPTER TWENTY-NINE

The fifth band — Red Yellow and Blue, from River City — is just about finished when Terence leads the PAQ to the stage.

"You ready?" says clipboard man over the chaotic noise of the Red Yellow and Blue, who have been thrashing around on stage, banging garbage can lids together and screaming at each other in what must be Martian.

"We're ready," Terence says.

"As soon as this . . . band," clipboard man shouts over the din, "finishes this . . . song, be ready to load in, all right?"

"Load in?" Eddie shouts back.

"Put your stuff on the stage and plug in," clipboard man explains.

He heads off to attend to clipboard-man business.

"Are we ready?" Terence says to his friends in a huddle behind the stage.

Novia nods and pats her harp case.

Claude cracks his knuckles. "Let's do this."

"Yeah, yeah," James says. "Pep talk, pep talk, blah blah. They're done. Let's get up there!"

"Um, hi," Eddie says into the mic to the smattering of a crowd at their feet. The speakers squeak in protest, and she backs off the mic a bit. "We're the PA Quintet, from Franklin Middle School, right here in town."

"And East High!" James says, leaning into her mic.

Eddie shoves him back to his gear. "Anyway, this one is a classic by Gerald Marks and Seymour Simons, from way back in 1931," she says into the mic.

A few people in the audience mutter and whisper.

"We've brought it out of the Stone Age," Eddie adds, smiling, and Claude plays the intro to "All of Me."

They play it slow and sparse. Eddie's vocals are powerful and rich, but slow and under control. James's beats suit her singing style, keeping everything laid back and cool, while Novia's hard playing gives the whole piece an eerie and almost mysterious air.

Terence couldn't be happier, and though he couldn't see Eddie's face from his position behind her, he could tell she was pleased too.

"That was amazing!" Eddie says as they climb down from the stage after the song.

"It was," Terence says, letting her throw her arms around his neck. "You were great."

"Hey, where's my hug?" Claude says. "I was great too."

The big eighth-grader throws his arms around Terence, and soon all five of the PA Quintet are in a group hug behind the stage.

"I have to admit," says Polly Winger as she and her band pass by on their way to take the stage. "That was good. You'll survive the round for sure."

"Don't sound so surprised," Eddie says, glaring at her.

Polly shrugs one shoulder. "I'm not," she says. "Honest." She flashes a big smile, climbs the steps to the stage, and steps up to the microphone.

"We're the Winger Five," she says, "from Hart Arts Academy here in River City. This one's called 'I'm Gonna Sit Right Down and Write Myself a Letter.'"

It's one that Terence taught her a year and a half ago. She'd never even heard of the Great American Songbook back then.

"Now look at her," Terence mumbles to himself.

"Do I have to?" Eddie says. She shrugs. "She's good."

"She is," Terence says.

"All right, all right," Eddie says. "She's great." She listens for a bit. "Do you have this song?"

"Of course," Terence says. "Actually, I have a recording of Polly singing it too."

Eddie sneers a bit, but then says, "Send it to me?"

Terence laughs. "You got it."

The PA Quintet survive the first round, as do the Winger Five. The second round begins at four, and this time the PAQ is up first.

Their rendition of "Now At Last" is cool and crisp, and while he's playing, Terence forgets it's warm outside today, even for spring.

The song and Eddie's voice are like a blanket of snow on a gray morning, James's beats and Novia's harp like the sun breaking through and reflecting off the snow, and Claude's piano playing like the cracking puddles underfoot. Terence hopes his bass is like the earth it all lies on top of.

The crowd is larger now, though Terence hardly notices until the song is finished and the crowd cheers.

The Winger Five play last in the second round. Polly steps up to the mic.

"Before we start," she says, "I just want to say thanks and good luck to all the other bands playing today — especially to the PA Quintet."

"What?" James says.

"If it weren't for Terence Kato," Polly goes on, "the Winger Five wouldn't even exist."

The audience slowly comes around and claps halfheartedly at Polly's urging.

"Now we're going to play 'Here Comes the Sun,'" Polly says, and she turns to the band to count them in.

"What was that all about?" Eddie says to Terence.

He can only shrug.

"Must be trying to throw you off," James says, leaning across Eddie to whisper to Terence. "Confuse you. She knows we'll be in the finals."

"Maybe," Terence says. It doesn't sound like something Polly would do, but maybe she's changed a lot since they used to hang out.

Polly bows after their rendition of the Beatles song, and she and her band leave the stage.

Clipboard man comes on clapping. "Weren't they great?" he says when he reaches the mic. "That was the Winger Five, and the last of our semifinalists this afternoon."

Clipboard man claps, and the crowd follows his lead with another round of applause.

"We're going to take five now," clipboard man goes on, "and I'll be back with the judges' choices for our three finalists. Sit tight."

"What do you guys think?" Terence asks when he and the rest of the PAQ have claimed a table in the shrinking green room.

"We're in," James says. "No doubt."

"I don't know," Novia says, drumming her long, skilled fingers on the green paper tablecloth. "Polly's band is really good, and those two bands from Upper Prince River were good too."

"That makes three," Eddie says.

"We were better than all of them," Claude insists, high-fiving James.

"Maybe," Terence says. "But Polly's band and us, we're both jazz. Or mostly jazz. What if they want a bigger variety?"

James crosses his arms. "We're not jazz."

Eddie cocks her head. "Um, we are though?"

James shakes his head. "We're trip-hop."

"Maybe," Terence says. "Not sure it's enough. The bands from Upper Prince are hard rock and country. It's like a lineup made for a final round: the perfect variety of American music."

The other fall silent and sit like that for a minute. Their anxious reverie is interrupted by clipboard man.

"All right, everyone," he says to the eight remaining acts, patting his clipboard. "I'm about to make the announcement. We've got the front rows set aside for you all."

"Good luck, Terence," Polly Winger says as she leads her band to the benches.

"You too," Terence says back, smiling.

"She's trying to throw you off," James hisses at him, but Terence ignores him.

When everyone is seated, clipboard man walks up to the mic. "I have here," he says, again patting his clipboard, "the names of the three acts that will perform right here in the finals tonight."

The crowd — made up of the eight surviving bands and their friends and families — cheers.

"First," clipboard man says, "from Upper Prince River, the Glass Banana!"

The hard rock four-piece jumps to their feet and high-five each other, and then run up on stage.

"And our second finalist," clipboard man goes on as the applause dies down, "from right here in River City . . ."

Terence leans forward and pumps his fists.

Clipboard man finishes, "The Winger Five!"

Terence sags, and quickly sits up straight and claps as Polly and her band walk onto the stage.

"And our last finalist today," clipboard man says.

Eddie grabs Terence's hand and squeezes it tight.

Clipboard continues, "Also from right here in River City . . ."

Terence is almost on his feet.

"The PA Quintet!"

Terence and his friends practically jump onto the stage, arms around each other in celebration.

He glances at Polly, who smiles at him across the stage and waves.

"In an hour," he says to Eddie, "one of us could be the champs of the battle."

Eddie looks across the stage at Terence's former bandmates. "And the other . . ."

"Won't be."

CHAPTER THIRTY

The PAQ are gathered at the bottom of the stage steps, ready to load-in.

"Guys," Eddie says, "it's not too late for us to play 'Shine a Light On' instead."

"Don't be ridiculous," Novia says. "We haven't played that in weeks."

"Besides," Terence says, "your song is going to kill."

Eddie takes a deep, fast breath between clenched teeth and looks up at the stage.

The Glass Banana is nearly finished with their third-round song — a 21 Pilots cover. It's good. If the judges are looking for a more marketable sound, these guys have it in the bag.

They finish up, bow quickly, and come down the steps past the PAQ.

"Good luck, you guys," the lead singer says.

"Thanks," Novia says. "You guys sounded great."

Eddie turns to Terence and takes him by both shoulders. "I need you to give me some confidence," she says, lowering her gaze.

Terence thinks for a minute, while onstage the clipboard man begins their introduction.

"Our next finalist," he announces, "is the Public Announcement Quintet, of River City."

"When I was new at Franklin Middle School," Terence says quickly, looking into Eddie's eyes, "you were the only person I wanted to see each day."

"Yeah?" she says.

"They got their first taste of local fame," the clipboard man goes on, "when their demo songs were played over the PA system at East High School."

Terence nods. "And when I heard your voice in the school basement that first day," he goes on, "I knew we were meant to play together and do something amazing."

"So please put your hands together," clipboard man says, "for the band better known as the PA Quintet!"

Eddie's nervous frown bends into a smile as the other band members head onstage to quickly set up.

"And we have," Terence finishes.

"OK," Eddie says, pulling him against her for a hug. "Let's do this."

Hand in hand, Eddie and Terence take the stage.

"I'm a little nervous about this," Eddie says into the mic, and the audience smiles and laughs and claps. "Our next song is . . . well, I wrote it."

The crowd is the biggest it's been all day, with Terence's dad, the Carsons, the Viateurs, the Paganos, and even James's parents in the front row. When *they* cheer, it spreads backward through the crowd until everyone is clapping and hooting — even Polly's Winger Five.

"Thank you," Eddie says, glancing at Terence. "It's called 'Within, Without.'"

She lowers her head as Novia starts the song. At the fourth bar, the rest of the band joins in, and then Eddie begins to sing at the next bar.

Her voice shakes — but just for the briefest instant. Terence notices; perhaps Polly will too. But quickly Eddie recovers, and her voice is under control, powerful and cool.

Terence has heard the song before, obviously, but this evening he closes his eyes and lets his fingers move on their own, and he listens. It's a song about what's inside her, and what she shows the world. In a way, though, it's a song about what's inside everyone.

Eddie holds the last note — a C at the top of her range — as long as she ever has, and before she even ends the song, the crowd is on their feet.

She bows, and she motions to the rest of the band. Terence bows too, and Claude gets up from his keyboard. Even James is smiling as he steps from behind the table he's got his laptop set up on to bow. Novia manages to awkwardly rise under the weight of the harp too, before Claude hurries over to help her stand.

The PAQ join hands and bow together, and then hurry from the stage.

"What is taking so long?" Eddie says, pacing in front of the stage.

"You have to relax," Claude says. "Have something to eat."

Eddie shakes her head. "I can't eat," she says.

Terence can hardly keep his seat too, and hasn't touched the Chinese takeout his father bought for the band after the third round.

"I don't know what you're so nervous about," James says, shoveling vegetable lo mein into his face.

"Yeah," Novia says. "Glass Banana probably won anyway."

"No!" Eddie says. "Don't say that!"

Novia shrugs. "Easier to expect the worse," she says. "Then if it doesn't happen, great! If it does, at least you were ready."

Terence watches clipboard man, who is sitting at a table with the judges: the owner of Wellstone Music Store, the talent booker at a famous downtown club, and a local entertainment blogger. They're in a heated debate, and Terence would love to go over and eavesdrop.

Soon, though, clipboard rises from the table and walks over to them. "Kids," he says, gathering the PAQ, the Winger Five, and the Glass Banana into a semicircle around him. "I'll be announcing the winner in ten minutes. Gather your friends and families!"

The PA Quintet sit together on one bench, huddling close as if they're watching the same horror movie.

Eddie takes Terence's hand. "I can't take it."

"I'm nervous too," Terence says, "but if we don't win, I think I'll be OK."

"Why?" Eddie says.

"Because I'm living my life," Terence says, smiling at her, "and I've got some great friends to do that with."

Eddie's expression softens as color rises in her cheeks.

Clipboard man finally takes the stage and steps up to the mic. "Before I announce this year's winner," he says, "I have to take a few minutes to thank all our sponsors."

An audible groan rises up from the crowd, but he goes on undeterred, listing the names of a dozen local businesses who supported the battle.

"And finally," he says, "to announce this year's winner. We had a great battle — the largest we've ever had, and every act who played today deserves a round of applause."

Everyone claps.

"I hope they'll all keep playing music," clipboard man says. "Today's first-place winner — the winner of recording studio time, a spot on the local bands compilation we produce each year with radio station SEBB-FM, and ten *thousand* dollars — is . . ."

They all lean forward on the bench.

"Glass Banana!"

They all sag together on the bench.

The four members of Glass Banana, arm in arm, hurry onstage to accept their award.

Terence is about ready to just get up and walk away, when clipboard man steps up to the mic again. "This year we have a special award, as well," he announces to settle down the crowd. A confused murmur rises up.

"Now, it took some special conniving at the judges'

table," he goes on with a chuckle, "but we came up with a great solution — and a special award for this year's best original song."

Eddie sits up.

Terence puts a hand on her arm. "Wait a second," he says. "Is he serious?"

Eddie's eyes go wide.

"Receiving a prize of recording studio time and a spot on our compilation," clipboard man says, "is the Public Announcement Quintet for their original song by Meredith Carson, 'Within, Without'! Come on up, PAQ!"

Together, the five bandmates run onstage to accept their impromptu award.

Terence looks out at the applauding crowd and finds his father, standing on a bench at the back so he can see over everyone's heads. He's grinning and clapping and shouting out Terence's name.

The five members of the PAQ join hands again to bow, and Terence realizes how happy he is. He's onstage with his four best friends, a group he never would have believed if he weren't a part of it.

For an instant, his heart hurts, because he's happy even though his mother is forever gone. But the instant passes quickly, and he reminds himself that this is the life his mother wanted for him: one filled with friends and music and joy.

And remembering her well means living it every day.

STEVE BREZENOFF

Steve Brezenoff is the author of more than fifty middle-grade chapter books, including the Field Trip Mysteries series, the Ravens Pass series of thrillers, and the Return to the Titanic series. He's also written three young-adult novels, *Guy in Real Life*; *Brooklyn, Burning*; and *The Absolute Value of -1*. In his spare time, he enjoys video games, cycling, and cooking. Steve lives in Minneapolis with his wife, Beth, and their son and daughter.